Running from the Past

Danger in Destiny
Book 5

Melanie D. Snitker

DALLIONE MEDIA, LLC

Running from the Past
Danger in Destiny: Book 5
By Melanie D. Snitker

All rights reserved
© 2024 Melanie D. Snitker

Dallionz Media, LLC
P.O. Box 5283
Abilene, TX 79608

Cover Art: Dallionz Media, LLC

Melanie D. Snitker
melanie@melaniedsnitker.com
www.melaniedsnitker.com

Rejoice always, pray without ceasing,
in everything give thanks;
for this is the will of God in
Christ Jesus for you.
1 Thessalonians 5:16-18

Chapter One

Peyton Kennedy's arms ached. She was well into the second straight hour of rocking and soothing her niece. She smoothed a hand over Rosie's dark, wispy hair. Every time she tried to lay the baby down in her crib, she would start crying again.

Rosie sneezed so loudly that it made Peyton jump. How could such a powerful sound come from such a tiny little body? She was only three months old, but the poor girl had a nasty cold that had her coughing, sneezing, and feeling downright miserable.

Peyton eyed the wall clock above the nursery door. As tired as her arms were, she didn't mind holding and comforting her niece. What she did mind was that her sister, Trina, was late. Again.

Part of Peyton's agreement to watch Rosie during the day while Trina worked was that Trina would be home by five o'clock so Peyton would have time to take a shower, get a bite to eat, and make it to her own job on time.

Working evenings and nights at a local grocery store

wasn't exactly glamorous—or what she'd imagined herself doing in her early thirties—but it paid the bills.

And she'd been late to her shift three times in the last two weeks. Her manager was going to have a fit if it happened again tonight, and Peyton couldn't afford to lose her job.

"Come on, Trina."

Rosie sneezed again and this time followed it with the cutest little half-coo, half-sigh.

Peyton chuckled quietly. "You poor sweetie."

She lifted the baby higher on her shoulder and patted her diapered bottom. It wasn't long before the little one finally started to relax.

"There we go." She began to sing a song she'd made up over the hours and hours of rocking her niece.

Even though she only sang the words, she could practically hear the piano accompaniment in her head. Her fingers ached to touch the keys. She hadn't played a piano in nearly two years, and it still felt wrong. One day, she'd save up enough money to buy another. Maybe she could quit her job stocking shelves at the grocery store and start teaching piano lessons again. It all felt like some far-off dream.

Peyton loved being here for Rosie, and she was glad that she could help Trina out. But this wasn't sustainable, not long-term.

Peyton's phone chimed with a text. Trying her best to not jostle the baby, she pulled her phone out to see that it was from Trina. She'd better not be running even later. Peyton squelched her frustration and opened the text.

"Stay in the nursery with Rosie until I come back and get you. Please. Love you."

She read it twice before typing back a response.

"Are you okay?"

There was no answering text. A thread of worry wound itself around her middle and squeezed.

When she heard the front door open five minutes later, she breathed a sigh of relief. She quietly swayed back and forth as she walked across the room toward the crib. She sent up a silent prayer that the baby would stay asleep for a while.

She expected Trina to come down the hall toward the baby's room until the sound of her voice carried from the other end of the house.

Peyton paused. She couldn't tell what was being said, but Trina's tone held a note of frustration. Maybe even worry.

Was she on the phone? Or had someone else come home with her? Was that why she was running so late?

Peyton tried to shove down her own irritation so Rosie didn't pick up on it. It wasn't the baby's fault her mother had terrible taste in men. Trina was forever dating someone new, and the guys were always less than stellar. Which, unfortunately, included Rosie's father.

It was a subject they'd argued about many times, and Peyton couldn't seem to get through to her sister. It would be better to remain single and focus on Rosie than to bounce from man to man. But Trina disagreed, and their arguments quickly shifted gears to focus on Peyton.

Trina liked to point out that since Peyton had gotten a divorce nearly two years ago, she was hardly in a position to offer relationship advice. And maybe the fact that her marriage with Jay had fallen apart did disqualify her from being an expert on it. But as far as quality men went? Jay was one of the good ones.

But marriage—life—had gotten hard. Instead of fighting for each other, they'd walked away. If Peyton could go back, she might have done things differently. She'd like to think *they* would have done things differently.

She shoved the regret and anger aside and tried to focus on her sister's voice as she eased Rosie into her crib.

A door slammed, and Peyton's gaze darted to the baby's face. She continued to sleep peacefully. Good. Hopefully, it would give Trina enough time to rest a little after work and allow Peyton to leave with enough time to change clothes before she started work herself.

She'd just reached the door and was about to step into the hallway when Trina's voice rose.

"I don't have it. You need to leave. Now."

There was a second, much deeper voice. Definitely a man, although Peyton couldn't make out what he was saying.

Trina's voice was firm. "No. She's not here. She's watching the baby at her place."

Peyton knew her sister well enough to detect an underlying nervousness in her tone.

Why was she lying about both Peyton and Rosie's location?

Something banged against a wall, startling Peyton.

Trina let out a strangled cry. "I told you. I don't know what you're talking about. I don't know where it is."

That deep voice again, loud enough to hear the murmur but quiet enough that the words weren't clear.

Peyton couldn't see anything from the hallway. She quietly crept forward, her right hand brushing the textured wall, and approached the living room. Worn beige carpet stretched from her shoes to the couch ahead. No one was visible.

Trina's voice rose. "They aren't here. They have nothing to do with this. Leave now."

A deep chuckle answered her. "I'm willing to bet if my friend here were to grab your kid, your memory would become a whole lot clearer."

Peyton covered a gasp. That meant there were at least two other people with Trina.

"No! Get out of my house. I'm calling the police."

The sound of a slap made Peyton jump. A cell phone fell to the floor in the living room and bounced on the carpet before landing near the hallway entrance just a few inches from her foot.

The deep voice rumbled. "Sit down. Now." He must have spoken to the other man in the room. "Go get the brat."

A chair scraped the ground, followed by a thud against the wall. Trina cried out, but her scream was cut short by a sickening thud.

A moment later, Trina's body slumped into view before collapsing in the middle of the living room floor. A large gash was visible on the right side of her temple.

Fear seized Peyton's heart, squeezing tightly and sending her pulse pounding in her ears.

Trina lay on the ground, facing Peyton, her dark eyes open but unseeing. Crimson spread from her lifeless body and soaked into the carpet around her.

It took everything in Peyton to keep her lips pressed together, holding her moans of disbelief and sorrow inside. Tears raced down her cheeks.

She bent down, snatched Trina's phone, and then whirled to run back to the nursery. Once inside, she locked the door. She stuffed the phone into her pocket.

Whoever killed Trina was still inside the house. Peyton

was sure of it. And this flimsy lock wasn't going to keep them out for long.

Maybe the killer would run away. If he did, then Peyton could give her sister CPR. Call an ambulance. Something.

Even as the thoughts flitted through her mind, she knew that it wouldn't do any good. There was no doubt in her mind that it was too late for Trina.

She took a steadying breath and willed her heart to stop racing. She could barely hear past the rush of blood in her ears.

Just when she was beginning to wonder if she and the baby were alone in the house, she heard the voice again.

"...a look around. There are only so many places to hide."

The words were uttered by the deeper voice from earlier, and it was followed by another one.

"Whether the sister and baby are here or not, we need to do a thorough search. Make it look like a robbery."

The deeper voice hadn't sounded familiar, but this second one? Peyton was certain she'd heard it somewhere but couldn't quite place it.

There were at least two people inside the house, and it was clear now that both were men. Whoever they were, Trina had lied to them about Rosie being there. But why? And what were they looking for?

Whatever it was, Peyton would be no use to Rosie if the intruders caught her. They knew Trina, yet they hadn't hesitated to kill her. They would do the same to Peyton.

She pushed the changing table in front of the door as quietly as possible, then grabbed the diaper bag and tossed Trina's phone inside. Next, she stuffed some diapers and wipes into the main compartment. She snatched a bottle that Rosie had emptied a short time earlier and threw it in along with the lone canister of formula sitting on the bottom shelf of the changing table.

After zipping the bag closed, she rushed to the window and kicked out the screen with a cringe, praying it didn't wake up the baby. She tossed the diaper bag outside. It landed on the grass below with a muffled thud.

She snagged a baby blanket and then carefully scooped Rosie into her arms.

Stay asleep. Stay asleep. Stay asleep.

The last thing she needed was for the baby to cry and draw attention to them. With any luck, the nursery wouldn't be the first place the intruders looked, giving Peyton some time to get away. She breathed a prayer of thanks when Rosie's little lips moved as though she were drinking milk, followed by a contented sigh.

The doorknob jiggled.

Peyton froze as goosebumps peppered her arms.

"Kick it in," the calmer voice commanded.

The changing table might slow them down, but it wouldn't stop them for long.

She dashed for the window. Climbing through it with a baby in her arms proved more challenging than Peyton thought it would be. Something caught her upper arm on the way out and tore her skin. She hissed with pain and nearly fell as she regained her balance on the uneven ground.

Rosie jerked, obviously startled by the change in posi-tion. But she settled back into Peyton's arms. With the diaper bag slung over one shoulder, she stuck to the dark shadows along the edge of the house.

The overgrown weeds and grass snagged at her pants and shoes as though they, too, were trying to prevent her escape.

Her old Honda was parked in front of the house. But right behind it was a car she didn't recognize. Did she dare run past it to get to hers? Would they hear the engine start up and come after her?

She felt the weight of Rosie cradled in her arms. More tears fell as she glanced at the drawn curtains that shrouded the front window. If they weren't in place, Peyton would be able to look in and see Trina's body on the floor...

She choked on a sob.

Rosie shifted in her sleep, reminding Peyton of the precious cargo she held. Trina had lied about Rosie being in the house. The last thing she did was try to protect her daughter.

Peyton needed to get her niece to safety. Then she would call the police, report what happened, and maybe they could catch the men before they even left the house. She awkwardly pulled her phone from her back pocket and took a picture of the unknown vehicle, making sure to get the license plate number in the frame.

A loud crash came from inside the house, followed by two more. Peyton jumped, and Rosie startled in her arms with a squeak.

As much as she wanted to be able to identify her sister's killers, she couldn't risk them seeing her. Couldn't risk getting caught.

She shoved her phone back in her pocket, took out her keys, and stuck to the shadows as she crouched. With a deep breath, she made a break for her car. By some miracle, she managed to get it unlocked without dropping the keys.

She tossed the diaper bag into the passenger seat, quickly placed Rosie in the floorboard—there was no time to strap her into her car seat in the back—and started the engine.

Her chest tightened. Her lungs burned as she forced herself to breathe normally and pulled away from the curb. She wanted to press the gas pedal and get away as fast as possible, but Rosie wasn't in her car seat, and she didn't want the men in the house to hear the engine.

"Please, Lord, help us get away. Keep Rosie safe."

Chapter Two

Peyton drove, slow and steady, down the street in front of her sister's house and took the first right. A glance in the rearview mirror assured her that no one was following them. At least not yet.

Tears blurred her vision. She blinked them away.

Rosie, awake and angry now, began to cry from the floorboard. Her wails filled the car, echoing the pain burning in Peyton's own heart.

"Shhhh. Rosie. I'm right here."

Her shaky words made no difference to the infant.

Peyton made her way through the neighborhood, past the next one, and to the small grocery store where she worked. She should be hurrying to change clothes so she could get to work on time. Instead, she pulled around behind the building, parked in the shadows, and turned the engine off.

She stretched across the console. It dug into her ribs as she reached for Rosie and awkwardly lifted her into her arms.

"Shhhh... Shhhh..."

Peyton pulled her phone out as she tried to calm her niece. It slipped through her fingers and fell onto the floorboard at her feet.

Rosie's eyes were scrunched closed, her face red, as she cried with everything that was in her.

"I know, sweetie. I know." Peyton lifted Rosie to her shoulder. The baby rubbed her wet face against Peyton's neck as she cried. Gradually, the screams turned to quiet cries and whimpers.

As soon as she was able, Peyton reached down and used her foot to push the phone toward her hand. Doing her best to rock back and forth in her seat, she dialed 9-1-1 and took a deep breath as the phone rang.

"9-1-1. What is the nature of your emergency?"

As if Rosie could sense the importance of the call, her quiet cries subsided, replaced with hiccups and a trembling lower lip.

"I need to report a murder." She gave the operator the address. "My sister, Trina Kennedy, was killed tonight. There were two men involved, but I don't know who they are. I did get a license plate number..."

"One moment, please."

Peyton blinked in surprise. She expected the operator to take the license plate number immediately. Or ask if she was safe. While she waited for the operator, she reached for a tissue and gently wiped the tears from Rosie's face and cleaned up her runny nose.

"Ma'am? Could I have your name and location please?"

"My name is Peyton Kennedy. I'm Trina's sister. The guys at the house started to search the place after they killed..." Her voice caught. "I had to leave. I'm not there right now." She could have told the operator her location, but something made her hesitate.

"Do you have a baby with you?"

She hadn't mentioned Rosie to the operator, but she'd probably heard Rosie crying when she first called, so there was no reason to hide the truth.

"My niece is here."

"A murder and kidnapping from the same location were called in five minutes ago. I need you to calmly bring the child to the nearest police department for questioning."

"What?" Peyton tried to digest the operator's words. They thought she'd kidnapped Rosie? The killers had to have called it in. There was no way anyone else in the neighborhood would have heard what happened.

"I didn't kidnap my niece. I'm trying to keep her safe."

"If that's true, then you need to hand her over to the authorities and turn yourself in. Cooperate, and we'll get everything sorted out."

She couldn't risk the police taking Rosie away from her as a precaution. Peyton was the only family she had now. And if they placed the baby with her father... Peyton shivered at the thought.

No. There had to be another way to figure out what was going on without risking Rosie's safety. Trina had died trying to protect her daughter, and Peyton would make sure it wasn't for nothing.

Peyton hung up the phone and tossed it into the cup holder.

If the operator was right, then the police might be looking for her already. They could come around the corner any minute. She had to get out of town. Go somewhere safe where they couldn't find her. Her own apartment wasn't an option. They were probably sending someone there right now. They might even set up an officer to wait in case she tried to hide out there.

Her thoughts turned to the men who had invaded Trina's home and killed her. If they truly were looking for Peyton now, they might be watching her apartment, too.

The fact that one of the killer's voices sounded familiar kept playing itself in the back of Peyton's mind. That meant she'd been around him at some point. Since she couldn't pinpoint where, it also meant that he could have been anywhere.

At the grocery store. The restaurant where Trina worked. Maybe even someone from her own apartment building.

Houston was a big city, but it suddenly seemed claustrophobic. She had no idea who she could trust, and it felt like everything was closing in on her.

She couldn't go home.

She had to assume the guys who killed Trina were coming after her, too. She didn't dare stop anywhere in town, not even to use her credit card to withdraw some money.

A fresh wave of fear rushed through her.

"I'm scared, God." The prayer was uttered in desperation as she tilted her head back and stared at the car's roof above her. "What am I supposed to do now?"

Her ex-husband's face immediately came to mind.

A combination of confusion, anger, and relief collided to form a ball of regret in her gut. The perfect emotional recap of their turbulent three-year marriage.

She'd moved to Houston to be near her sister, or at least that was her excuse. Truthfully, she'd wanted to put some distance between herself and Jay. That way, she wouldn't run into him on a regular basis like she would have if she'd stayed in his hometown of Destiny, Texas.

She stared at her phone. Did he have the same number?

If she called and asked him to come get them, would he? Would he even hear her out if she showed up on his doorstep?

The thought of seeing him now sent waves of anxiety rolling through her. But she needed help. *Rosie* needed help.

For better or worse, Jay was the only person Peyton could think of who might know what to do.

What should have been less than a four-hour drive to Destiny turned into a much longer ordeal. It was three in the morning now, and Peyton was exhausted. They'd barely driven an hour when Rosie had a blowout. The mess had managed to escape the baby's onesie and get all over the car seat.

Peyton had to pull into a rest stop, carry the car seat into the restroom, and do her best to clean it up. She'd practically had to give Rosie a bath in the sink before she was clean enough to get her dressed in a new outfit.

Now they were barely another hour down the road, and Rosie was screaming from the backseat. Peyton focused on the road ahead of her as a headache pounded behind her eyes.

A sign indicated a roadside park ahead. Just the thought of pulling over in the middle of the night made Peyton nervous, but she needed to see what was wrong with Rosie. She found a parking spot beneath a bright streetlight.

She got out of the car and climbed into the back next to the car seat. "What's the matter, sweetie?"

Rosie's face was bright red. She shoved her own fist in

her mouth and sucked on it only to flail her arm with another round of crying.

The baby was hungry. Peyton tried to remember when she last fed her niece and couldn't. She awkwardly made a bottle using the canister of formula she'd brought along with a bottle of water. When the bottle was ready, she unlatched the car seat and lifted Rosie into her arms.

She felt especially warm. Was she running a fever?

Peyton shoved down her growing concern. She hoped Rosie was just overheated from all the crying.

The baby accepted the bottle hungrily. As she drank, she snorted through her congested nose.

Peyton leaned back and tried to relax for the sake of her niece.

Her stomach gave an angry rumble. There wasn't a single thing in the car for her to eat. She could see a vending machine under a covered area not far away. Unfortunately, she had no cash on her. She didn't usually carry much, but she'd used what little she had the day before. What she wouldn't give for enough change to get a candy bar right now.

Her eyes grew heavy, and she blinked to stay focused.

Rosie finished her bottle, and Peyton lifted her to her shoulder. She rubbed the baby's back until she burped, then strapped her back into the car seat. She tried not to worry about how warm the little one still felt.

Rosie fussed about being placed in the car seat, and a pang of guilt went through Peyton. "I'm sorry, but we have to get going again."

She fought back tears as she climbed behind the wheel and pulled away from the roadside park while Rosie screamed from the back seat.

Chapter Three

D r. Jay Baird made a note on his tablet and looked up at his patient. Vincent McNight was in his late sixties and incredibly fit for his age. As a mail carrier, he got more than his fair share of exercise, which was probably why his knee had been acting up lately. Hopefully, using a light brace for support would be all he needed to keep the discomfort at bay.

Jay wished all his senior patients were so active and in such good shape. "If you find the brace isn't giving you enough support, or if you have any other trouble, just call up front, and we can look at other options."

"I appreciate that, Doc." Vincent reached out and shook hands. "I don't know what I'll do if I ever get to the point where I'm laid up at home." He stood from the examination table.

"I completely understand. Hopefully, that won't be an issue for a long, long time. Try the brace, and let me know how it goes." Jay stood and walked his patient to the door. "Have a great day. Enjoy the beautiful weather."

"You do the same." With a nod, Vincent entered the hallway and followed the signs to the front desk, where he could check out.

Jay glanced at the window. It was Friday and not even nine in the morning. The weather was often pretty warm in their area of Texas in September. But this weekend, it was supposed to be cooler than normal. It was the perfect start to his week-long vacation. The clinic was only open until noon on Fridays. Then he'd be free to head home.

He hadn't taken a proper vacation since...

Thoughts of the trip he and Peyton had taken to Colorado flitted through his mind. It was the year before things fell apart between them. They spent a week skiing, staying bundled up around a roaring fire, and reconnecting after his nine-month deployment.

Or at least he thought they were reconnecting. It turned out that the vacation and time together had been a tiny bandage covering a much larger wound. One neither of them knew how to heal. It was a relief when he was deployed again, and that realization had brought along with it a great deal of guilt.

He preferred to stay busy. Focused on work and his patients.

As much as he needed this week off, he dreaded the extra time it would give him to think. He should have arranged a camping trip with some friends. Bryce wouldn't be able to do anything last minute since his wife, Megan, was due with their first baby in less than two months. But maybe Nate would be available. He'd call after lunch.

His appointment with Vincent didn't take long, giving him fifteen minutes before his next patient. Jay headed for his office to make a few notes and check his messages. He'd barely taken a step in that direction when Cassie, one of the nurses at Destiny Family Medical, ran up behind him.

"Dr. Baird? I'm sorry to bother you, but I've got a patient waiting in exam room two." Her gaze shot to the closed door of the room she spoke of, and she lowered her voice. "She insisted on being worked into your schedule."

He blinked in surprise. "Mine specifically?"

"Yes. Refused to leave until we let her through. She seems to feel okay, but she's got an infant that is sick."

"Is she or the baby currently a patient with us?"

"No. And she preferred to speak to you about what was going on. I didn't get any vitals."

They usually tried to work established patients in when they could. But there was rarely room for someone who came in with no appointment or prior notification.

Except that, with Vincent leaving early and Jay's next patient not scheduled for another fifteen minutes, he did have time for a quick stop.

"I'll take care of it. Thank you, Cassie."

She seemed relieved as she bobbed her head. "You're welcome."

Outside of room two, he picked up the incredibly thin file that rested in the hanger on the door. At least they'd insisted on getting the patient's personal and contact information.

He flipped it open and took in the name.

Rosie Kennedy. The baby was barely three months old.

Normally, most people take young children to pediatricians instead of bringing them to their family clinic. Not that it didn't happen.

He'd make sure the infant was okay and refer the mother to a local pediatrician, and hopefully that would be that.

His attention stalled on the last name, reminding him of another Kennedy. A beautiful woman whom his life revolved around. Until it didn't.

Shoving thoughts of his ex-wife from his mind, he used one finger to push his wire-rimmed glasses higher on his nose. He opened the door and stepped inside.

"Good morning. I'm Doctor—"

The words died on his lips when the very person he'd been trying not to think about seemed to materialize before his eyes.

Peyton. The woman he'd fallen in love with. Married. Thought he'd spend the rest of his life with.

She'd left town shortly after the divorce was finalized, and he hadn't spoken to her or seen her since. It'd been nearly two years. He'd heard that she had reverted to her maiden name.

He took in her pretty face and the nervous look in her green eyes. It was those expressive eyes that had drawn him to her in the first place. No matter what was going on between them, she'd never been able to hide her thoughts from him. Even if she'd carefully kept her expression neutral, he could tell by her eyes what she was thinking. Feeling. Or at least that used to be the case.

She'd changed her hair. It used to be nearly waist-length but was now bobbed just above her shoulders—a visible indication of many more changes that remained unseen.

He inhaled and was immediately struck by a scent that transported him back in time. The combination of vanilla and something uniquely Peyton made him realize how much he'd missed it. He remembered when the scent no longer lingered in the house after she'd left.

He forced his gaze to the baby girl in Peyton's arms.

Apparently, Peyton had moved on since leaving Destiny.

Of course, she had. He shouldn't be surprised. But why was she here now? And why, of all the doctors in all the clinics in town, did she come to him?

"Peyton." He greeted her with a nod and then turned his attention to the baby. "This must be Rosie."

The baby fussed and sneezed. Peyton took a tissue out of her pocket and wiped away the generous amount of discharge that had escaped from the baby's nose.

There was no missing the family resemblance. Rosie had the same dark hair and dainty ears. Her eyes were brown instead of green, though. And her hair had some waves in it, unlike Peyton's.

His heart gave a painful twist. There'd been a time when he could picture Peyton holding *their* child. He'd even imagined a little girl who looked just like her. He swallowed hard and tried to push this new round of thoughts from his head.

Why had Peyton asked for him? To prove that she'd moved on after they'd gone their separate ways? He wouldn't have thought her capable of that, but he knew all too well how quickly people—and situations—could change.

He glanced at her left hand. No wedding ring or even a tan line where one might have been. Not that it meant anything definitively.

He shoved his tangle of emotions into a mental box, slammed the lid, and pulled his professional smile into place.

"How long has Rosie been sick?"

"This is the fifth day." Peyton shifted the baby to sit on her knee and let her lean against her chest. "She seems to be feeling worse, not better."

"Any fever? Vomiting?"

"No vomiting. No fever until this morning."

Her voice was tight with worry.

Jay carefully kept his attention on the baby as he listened to her lungs, felt her tiny lymph nodes, and looked at her ears, nose, and throat.

If he could stay focused on his young patient, then he could get through this appointment, and Peyton would be on her way again.

Jay made several notes in Rosie's chart. "If you don't have a humidifier, I'd recommend getting one. It'll help keep the air moist and make it easier for her to breathe. You can use a bulb to suction out her nose, and saline spray can help clear it and give some relief."

"What do I do if her fever gets worse? Or she starts coughing more?"

"Hopefully, this is just a cold that will pass soon." He gave her a list of conditions and changes she should look for. "If you see anything like that, you should take her back to her pediatrician or into urgent care for another evaluation."

He touched the baby's head. She really was adorable. Did Peyton look like this when she was little?

"I hope she feels better soon." He'd turned to leave the room.

"Jay? Wait," Peyton blurted.

He paused, his back to her. He considered leaving anyway, but there was something about her voice. She sounded vulnerable. Almost scared.

He slowly pivoted to face her again, his expression carefully neutral. "I'm more than happy to see your daughter and make sure she's doing well. She's beautiful, by the way. But the small talk—I've got other patients waiting, some who have had appointments scheduled for weeks. I wish you and Rosie nothing but the best."

He was about to turn to leave again when something on Peyton's sleeve snagged his attention. He stepped closer. There was no mistaking the dried blood that smeared her sleeve on the side of her arm. "Are you hurt?"

"I need your help. I didn't know where else to go."

Chapter Four

The first thing Peyton noticed when Jay walked into the examination room was that he sported facial hair. He'd always kept his face clean-shaven before. The mustache and goatee gave him a rugged appearance. It was a good look for him. Really good.

Her attention dropped to his leg. He barely had a limp. In fact, if someone wasn't looking for it, she doubted they would notice it at all. When they'd divorced, he was still using a crutch to get around most of the time.

After what she'd just told him, she half expected him to walk out of the exam room and not look back. If their situation had been reversed, and he asked for help after nearly two years of not speaking, she might have been tempted to do the same thing.

She watched as his shoulders lifted and his back straightened. He didn't respond immediately, but he fixed his dark eyes on her as though he were trying to read her thoughts. Her emotions.

There was a time when he knew her better than anyone

else. Peyton wanted to mourn that connection, but there was too much at stake right now.

He looked from her wounded arm to her face, his expression shifting from concern to anger. "What's going on? Did someone hurt you?"

"It's a long story. I'll tell you everything, but it'll take a while."

He ran a hand over his short, dark brown hair and shook his head. "I have other patients waiting. Where are you staying? I only work a half day on Fridays. I can try to come by at lunch."

At the mere mention of lunch, her stomach growled. She hoped he didn't hear it. She hesitated. "My car. I can stay in the parking lot. Come back in when you're on your lunch break. Or you can come out."

She started telling him which car it was, but the shocked look on his face silenced her.

"You're staying in your car?" His voice sounded doubtful. Incredulous. His gaze took in the diaper bag at her feet. "Please tell me this isn't everything..." But he must have been able to tell by her expression that all she had was in the examination room with them.

"I told you, it's a long story." She shifted Rosie in her arms and focused on the baby's face. At least she was content for now.

He was silent for several moments, probably thinking through his options. Finally, he extended an arm in her direction and motioned toward the doorway.

"You can wait in my office. I'll have a portable crib brought in. Make yourself comfortable, and once I'm caught up with patients, you can tell me this long story of yours."

Peyton hated needing anything from anyone, and that was especially true when it came to Jay. But right now, she didn't have a choice. If it were just her, things would be different. But she was responsible for Rosie now.

"Thank you."

The tension in her shoulders eased a little as she followed him down the hall to his office. It was a generous space with a wooden desk, an ergonomic chair, and a line of file cabinets along one wall. There was a simple couch against another. A large window let in plenty of sunlight, making the room feel airy and inviting.

Overall, the office was functional and comfortable. It fit Jay's personality perfectly.

"I'll be right back."

With that, he disappeared, coming back moments later with a folded portable crib. He set it up for her, then nodded toward the small refrigerator that was next to the filing cabinets. "There's water in there. Help yourself. I'll be back as soon as I can. My last patient is at eleven thirty, but sometimes the schedule runs late."

"It doesn't matter. We'll be fine, and this is much more comfortable than the car. Thank you."

There were a million questions reflected in his gaze as he gave a final nod and left the office, closing the door behind him and shutting out the bustle of the clinic.

Peyton dropped the diaper bag onto the couch and sank into it with a sigh of relief. Just because Jay offered the shelter of his office for the morning didn't mean he was going to help them once he knew why she was there.

What if he turned her away? Or even worse, what if he took it upon himself to call the police and let them know where she was?

There were a lot of uncertainties, but for the first time since she'd fled Trina's house, Peyton felt safe even if that safety would only extend for the next handful of hours.

Rosie started to fuss and attempted to shove her whole fist into her mouth.

"I know, sweetie. I know." She used the last of the water in the diaper bag, combined it with formula, and mixed up a bottle. Thank goodness she'd found the canister of formula in the nursery. She prayed it'd be enough to get them through until she could get to the store.

"Peyton?"

She barely registered the words until a light touch to her arm had her catapulting to her feet.

"Whoa!" Jay took a step back, his hands raised. "I didn't mean to startle you."

It took a breath or two for Peyton to remember that she was in his office at the clinic. She glanced at the portable crib, relieved to see that Rosie was still sleeping.

She checked her watch for the time. Almost noon. She and Rosie had been sleeping for two hours. Peyton hadn't even heard Jay come back into the office. What if it'd been someone else? What if the guys from Trina's house had somehow tracked her here?

She didn't realize her breaths were coming so quickly until Jay took her elbow and guided her back to the couch. Black spots danced in front of her eyes.

"You're hyperventilating. Take some deep breaths." He crouched in front of her. "In... Out... In... Out... Good."

Peyton nodded as the panic subsided and her vision cleared. She settled her elbows on her knees and cradled her head in her hands. "I'm sorry. I wasn't sure where I was at first." The reason sounded lame, even to her.

To Jay's credit, he said nothing as he claimed a spot on the couch beside her.

Her stomach chose that moment to growl so loudly that when she lifted her head, she found him watching her, one eyebrow raised.

"When was the last time you ate?"

She intended to grab a snack at Trina's house but never did. Then, the plan was to eat something quick at her house before going to work. She bit her lower lip and tried to shove images of Trina out of her mind.

"Lunch. Yesterday."

If her answer surprised him, he didn't show it.

A quiet knock sounded from the door. He stood and opened it, accepted a bag, and closed the door again.

He turned and held it up.

Peyton sucked in a breath when she saw the Corner Café logo. Her stomach let loose with another long growl, but she couldn't even be embarrassed.

Jay took out a wrapped burger and handed it to her. "Lettuce, tomato, mustard. Unless things have changed." He paused.

When she shook her head and took it gratefully, he handed her a container of fries.

"Thank you."

He took out his own burger and fries, got them both a bottle of water from his mini fridge, and rejoined her on the couch. "You're welcome. Best burgers in Destiny."

Peyton took a bite and groaned. She shook her head as she swallowed. "Uh-uh. Best burgers in Texas." She didn't even bother with the fries until her burger was half gone.

It'd been one of her favorite places to eat when she lived in Destiny. She and Jay had eaten at Corner Café many times, including on their first date. She'd always associated the place with him.

Only then did she realize Jay was watching her, a concerned look on his face.

Her cheeks warmed.

"Peyton. What's going on?"

Any appetite that remained immediately evaporated. She set the rest of her burger on the wrapper and took a long drink of water.

Jay followed suit, setting his burger aside and giving her his full attention.

She took in a steadying breath. "My sister? Trina?" Just mentioning Trina's name caused tears to flood her eyes. "Someone killed her last night, and by now, I'm probably a suspect. I didn't know where else to go."

Chapter Five

Jay had considered several scenarios that might explain why Peyton had shown up at his clinic. Abusive boyfriend. Car accident. But her fleeing from a murder scene and possibly being a suspect hadn't even entered the equation.

He waited, half expecting her to laugh and give him the real reason she was there.

Instead, she stared at him, her green eyes wide. A tear escaped and slid down her cheek, only to be brushed away with one of her slender fingers. He noticed, for the first time, a tiny heart tattoo on her right wrist. She'd always sworn she would never get a tattoo. What, or who, had changed her mind?

He stood, gathered the rest of his food, and tossed it in the wastebasket by his desk. When he turned to face her again, he slid his hands into the pockets of his jeans. "I think you'd better give me the unabridged version."

As though she'd been waiting for her cue, Rosie shifted and started to fuss.

Jay watched as Peyton abandoned her food and stood to scoop the baby into her arms.

She patted her back and swayed gently. "Rosie is Trina's daughter. My niece."

He didn't want to analyze why that revelation flooded his system with relief.

"I watch her during the day while Trina works. Worked." She swallowed hard and blinked rapidly. "Then Trina came home in the evening, and that's when I started my job." She lifted the baby and pressed a kiss to her cheek.

Taking care of an infant was a full-time job on its own. When did she sleep? He didn't voice the question, not wanting to interrupt her.

"Rosie has been sick, and I was trying to get her to calm down and go to sleep last night when Trina texted me, telling me to keep Rosie in her room." Her voice caught, and fresh tears filled her eyes. "She came home, but she wasn't alone. There were two guys that I could hear. I don't know if they were invited, or if they followed her. But they argued, and then there was a struggle. Trina collapsed. I'm not sure how they killed her..." Her eyes slid closed, and she held the baby to her chest.

Jay took a step toward her, and reached out, but let his arms fall to his sides again. "I can't even imagine."

"Trina was lying on the floor. A cut on her head. Staring. There was so much blood."

She continued to hold Rosie close, swaying back and forth as though the baby could be a buffer between herself and the memories she seemed reluctant to relive.

"The two guys were looking for something. All I knew was that if they were willing to kill Trina, they wouldn't hesitate to kill me, too. So I ran back to the nursery and locked and barricaded the door. Took what I could fit in the diaper bag, and we went out the window." She lifted her arm—the one with blood on the sleeve. "That's how I scratched myself."

He resisted the urge to ask to see her arm. To make sure she was okay. It seemed like a lot of blood for a scratch. "Why didn't you call the police?"

"I did. Rosie was crying in the background. The operator said someone had reported the murder and a kidnapping, and she wanted me to turn myself in immediately." She shifted Rosie so that she could see the baby's face. Her eyes lifted, her gaze connecting with his. "This was ten minutes or less after I left the house. It had to be one of the guys there who called..." She swallowed hard. "I couldn't... Rosie is all the family I have left."

Her words weren't meant as a barb, but they lodged themselves in his skin and stung all the same. There was a time when they were family. The two of them. When he couldn't imagine living his life without her.

A lot had changed in nearly two years.

"Where's Rosie's father?"

Peyton shook her head. "That's an even longer story."

Rosie stretched and fussed some more. Peyton pulled her keys from a front pocket and dangled them in front of the baby, who awkwardly grasped them.

"So you drove from..."

"Houston."

"You drove from Houston to Destiny. To ask me for help."

When she nodded her agreement, Jay ran a hand through his close-cropped hair, his nails scraping his scalp.

"If you won't go to the cops, I don't know what you expect me to do. Why did you come to me?"

Disappointment brought her chin down, and Jay could have kicked himself for it.

"Because you're the first person I thought of." Her lashes lifted, and the vulnerability in her green eyes snagged him and held him hostage.

It'd been impossible to deny those beautiful eyes from the moment he first met Peyton. Divorced or not, he still had no effective defense against them. A big part of him wanted to ask her to leave, while another wanted to pull her close and try to figure out what was happening.

Instead, he withdrew his phone and typed in specific search words to see what he could find about Trina's death. His heart ached thinking about what it must have been like for Peyton to witness her sister's murder.

He had a brother himself. And while they weren't overly close, if someone had hurt Sam, Jay would've gone to any lengths to get justice. How could he fault Peyton for doing the same thing for her sister?

To his surprise, there wasn't a single mention of the murder. Another search came back with nothing as well. That made no sense. Usually, something like that would be all over the news by now.

Peyton retrieved a rattle from her bag and handed it to Rosie, pocketing her keys again. "Did you find something about Trina? It's bad, isn't it? I can tell."

"It's confusing because there's not a single mention of Trina's death anywhere. Not on social media, not in the morning newspaper."

"What?" Her brows drew together in confusion. "I don't understand. How can there not be? The lady in the 9-1-1 office made it sound like they were going to send out a search party if I didn't turn myself in." The anxious tone of her voice brought Rosie's attention to her aunt. Peyton distracted the baby with the rattle and calmed her tone. "Why weren't the police sent to Trina's house?"

"Maybe it was meant to scare you. Maybe they called in and said it was a mistake or a prank. Maybe they were looking for something." Jay tilted his head toward Rosie. "But you grabbed her first."

Peyton's eyes widened as she studied the infant in her arms. A moment later, she shook her head. "I don't think so. It sounded like they were going to use Rosie to make Trina give them something else. Rosie's father isn't in the picture. It'd be one thing if they kidnapped her themselves and were going to use her as ransom, but when they killed Trina..." Her voice cracked. "Maybe they're trying to keep it out of the press for some reason. Surely the police were called in and found some kind of evidence. The murder weapon. Something. I don't even own a gun."

She walked to the couch and sat down, placing Rosie on her lap. "Whatever happens, I can't let them take Rosie away. I need to find a way to disappear. People do that all the time, right? Come up with a new identity and disappear?"

A sense of panic bubbled up at the thought of her trying to leave town under these circumstances. Her odds of successfully disappearing were low unless she knew who to contact. Then, she'd spend the rest of her life looking over her shoulder.

And he'd spend the rest of his wondering if she'd made it. If she was okay.

"Peyton, this isn't something you can just run away from."

The moment the words were out of his mouth, pain flashed in her eyes. Regret settled in his stomach like rotten food. Her instinct, when faced with a difficult situation, was to run in the opposite direction. Avoid it completely if she could. The very topic had come up in numerous discussions surrounding their divorce.

It was pretty messed up that he'd used those same words on her again. "I didn't mean that. I'm sorry. I worded that poorly. What I should have said is that we need to know more about the situation so you don't have to worry about losing Rosie or putting yourself in danger." He waited until she looked at him. "Is the car outside yours? Is it registered in your name?"

"Yes. It's mine."

If the police truly were searching for Peyton, there would be a BOLO out on her car. "If a police officer scans your license plate, they'll know where you are. This parking lot is going to start emptying soon, and your car will be easier to spot. We need to get it out of sight."

She frowned, a flicker of regret on her face. "While I was driving here, I wished I were one of those people who had enough money lying around to dump the car and pay cash for a different one. Hitchhiking was out of the question since I didn't know if they'd put my picture on the news or not."

Jay's eyes widened. "I'd like to hope you'd have the good sense not to hitchhike no matter what the situation. It'd be better to call someone to come get you than to do that."

"Like you?" There was a challenging edge to her voice. "If I'd called you, would you have come to Houston to pick us up? I haven't heard from you in almost two years, Jay."

"The phones work in both directions. I haven't heard from you, either."

She didn't argue. She couldn't because it was the truth. They both knew it.

It was as if, once they'd both signed the divorce papers,

all strings had been cut. Several of Jay's friends had commented on how their divorce was one of the strangest they'd been witness to.

If she had called, instead of showing up on his doorstep, and asked for help, would he have driven to Houston for her?

Without hesitation.

"I need to tie up a few loose ends. Then you can follow me to my house. We'll hide your car in the garage."

She reached out and snagged his hand. "Does this mean you're going to help me?"

He couldn't possibly count how many times he'd held her hand in his. Walks in the park, watching a movie together, and even while mourning the loss of a close friend. That simple connection was one they'd shared often, and it was one he'd missed immensely after they went their separate ways.

"Let's take this one step at a time."

He didn't even know if it was possible to get her out of this mess.

But, Heaven help him, he wouldn't be able to live with himself if he didn't try.

Chapter Six

There was some relief as Peyton watched the overhead door close. The cluttered two-car garage grew dark as the door shut out the sunshine, effectively hiding her Honda from the world. A lungful of air escaped her.

"Come on." Jay took the diaper bag from her. "I wasn't expecting company, so you'll have to excuse the mess."

There was no missing the tinge of humor and maybe sarcasm in his voice. He especially hadn't been expecting to be bringing her to his house.

It wasn't exactly something she'd envisioned twenty-four hours ago either.

As she'd driven up the driveway and into the garage, she'd been struck by how normal it looked. A brick house with a manicured lawn, all set in the middle of a cozy neighborhood.

She followed him into the kitchen with Rosie safely nestled in her arms. The baby sneezed and coughed as the overheated garage air gave way to cool air conditioning.

There were dishes piled in the sink, but the kitchen

itself was clean. The scent of lemons collided with dish soap and something else she couldn't quite identify.

Jay flipped on lights as he led her through the kitchen and a cozy living room. Her attention was immediately drawn to the upright piano against the far wall. It was the very same piano they'd had in their home before the divorce.

Peyton had no idea he'd kept it. She assumed he'd sold it the moment he could. After all, he didn't know how to play, and while it wasn't an overly high-end piano, it wasn't a cheap one, either.

She'd spent hours at that piano, filling their home with music. She'd taught occasional lessons and dreamed of turning that into a real job someday.

That dream, along with so many others, had faded away. In fact, it was the last piano she'd touched. Her fingers tingled at the thought, and she clenched her free hand into a fist as she followed Jay to a hallway on the other side of the living room.

The first room they passed was clearly set up as an office with a desk, bookcases, and a TV. A small bathroom was next, followed by a bedroom.

Jay turned that light on and motioned for Peyton and Rosie to go in ahead of him.

There was a queen-sized bed, a short dresser, and a variety of bookcases filled with movies and books. It wasn't a large room, but it was warm. Homey. The bedspread was light blue—Trina's favorite color. Peyton blinked back tears.

Jay shrugged. "I keep this room available for the occasional visit from my parents or Sam and Candace. You can use it for Rosie if she needs a nap. Or if you need to rest yourself."

"I appreciate it."

The air between them was thick with unspoken words. She wasn't sure if he was offering her a place to stay for the day, the night, or until she got her situation back under control.

"As soon as I know it's safe to access my bank account, I'll find somewhere else to stay. Or maybe traveling outside Texas would be better."

She pulled her bottom lip between her teeth.

Without hesitation, he reached out and touched her lip with his thumb. It used to be a gentle reminder not to damage it with all her worrying. A loving reaction that often calmed her. Reminded her that she wasn't fighting something alone.

Except that's exactly what she'd been doing for nearly two years now.

He dropped his hand immediately and took a step back, clearly as shocked by his instinctive reaction as she was.

"Sorry," he muttered.

Her heart thumped in response, but she managed to shrug as though it weren't a big deal. "Old habits."

He set the diaper bag on the bed. "I need to grab some things from my car. I'll be back in a few minutes."

With that, he walked out leaving Peyton alone with Rosie. She kissed the baby on her cheek and frowned at the feel of her warm skin against her lips. "We're quite a pair, Rosie girl. What are we going to do?"

Once outside, Jay leaned against his car and took in a deep breath. The end of their marriage had been devastating on multiple levels. He'd been struggling with PTSD, something he hadn't truly shared with her, along with a long recovery from a wound he'd received while on deployment. It wasn't until after their divorce that he'd finally sought help the way he should have from the beginning.

It signaled the start of his healing. And it also brought into his life several individuals that he'd come to see as friends. People he could call on, who understood what it was like to survive something traumatic like he had while he'd been deployed.

Having Peyton here, and under his roof, was enough to deal with. But trying to unearth what was happening to her while potentially protecting both her and Rosie?

There was a lot of information that was going to be difficult for Jay to get a hold of. But he happened to know someone he'd gone through group therapy with that he was certain would be able to lend a hand.

Jay pulled his phone out and dialed Nate's number. His friend answered on the second ring.

"Hey, J-Man. What's going on? You finally free?"

Nate knew about Jay's vacation. In fact, before Peyton had dropped back into his life, he'd intended to see if Nate was up for a camping or fishing trip this weekend. Now, he wasn't sure what the week ahead held.

"Yep. I've been off work for thirty minutes, and I've got a situation on my hands."

"What can I do?" Nate's tone had moved from joking to somber.

"Peyton's back in town, and she's in trouble. I'm not going to lie, brother. She witnessed a murder, and the police may be charging her with murder and kidnapping. It's a serious mess, so I completely understand if you don't want to—"

"Where are you guys now?"

"My house."

"I'll be there in ten." The call ended with a click.

Knowing Nate was on the way eased some of Jay's worry. He quickly dialed another friend's number. There was a good chance Bryce might not answer. His schedule as a firefighter was constantly in flux. But thankfully, he responded quickly.

"Jay. Good to hear from you."

"Hi, Bryce. How's Megan doing?"

"She's well. Thanks for asking. What can I do you for?"

"Am I remembering right that your sister is in charge of a church clothing ministry of some kind?" Jay was sure the conversation had come up at some point.

"Erica. Yeah, she was. I think she's transitioned it to the church full-time. I can give her a call and see what's going on with that. What do you need?"

"Whatever I can get for a three-month-old baby girl. I also need a change of clothes and some pajamas for a woman. Size twelve pants, medium shirt."

There was a pause, and Jay imagined Bryce writing down the information.

"Got it. Everything okay?"

"Yeah. Peyton's back in town, and she's gotten herself into some trouble."

"I'm sorry to hear that. You guys need some help? Say the word..."

Jay smiled. "I appreciate it. I think we're okay for now. I need to keep Peyton's return on the down-low. We could use some prayers for clarity and guidance, though."

"Absolutely. I won't say a word, but we'll be praying. And I'm serious, Jay. I never got the chance to pay you back for patching Megan up. I'm happy to return the favor."

Two years ago, Megan had sustained a burn in a fire that was supposed to kill her. Bryce was trying to find the person responsible and keep her safe when her burn became infected. Jay had cleared an appointment slot and treated the burn.

"You don't owe me a thing. The prayers are huge on their own. Thanks again."

"No problem. I'll have someone bring the clothes to you. Tell Peyton I said hey."

"Will do."

Jay hung up and pocketed his phone before opening the trunk of his car. He retrieved a cardboard box and carried it inside. After locking the front door again behind him, he took the box to the guest room and dropped it on the bed with a plop.

Peyton eyed the box. "What's that?"

Instead of explaining, he opened the flaps and let the contents speak for themselves.

One of the perks of being in the medical field was receiving an enormous amount of sample items from different companies. It came in handy when he had a patient who needed to try a different type of formula or medication.

In this case, he'd brought home diapers, wipes, and several canisters of formula. He wasn't sure how much Peyton had, but if the diaper bag was her only possession, it couldn't be much.

She pinched the bridge of her nose and blinked rapidly. "Jay... This is amazing. Thank you."

"You're welcome." He nodded toward her arm. "I've got a fully stocked first aid kit in the bathroom. Can I take a look at your arm? Make sure it's okay?"

She looked down at her arm as though she'd completely forgotten about the wound. "It's fine. Really." She wrinkled her nose in a way that was entirely too distracting. "Right now, I've got a minor emergency that needs to be addressed."

The pungent smell wafted to Jay's nose. "No joke." He reached out and softly rubbed the top of one of Rosie's hands.

The doorbell went off, and Peyton jumped. Her eyes darted to the bedroom door.

"It's okay," he assured her. "It's a friend. He's here to help us."

"No! What if he turns me in? Or says something to the wrong person?"

"He won't." She was about to speak again when he placed a hand on her shoulder and gave it a gentle squeeze. "I can keep you and Rosie hidden here, and we can do some general investigating. But we need help, and I need you to trust me."

Chapter Seven

It took some time for Peyton to get Rosie cleaned up. The baby had had another blowout, and the mess had gone halfway up her back. By the time Peyton was done wiping it up, Rosie was crying full force.

"I know you're cold. And mad." She finished getting everything under control and then lifted her niece into her arms. "There we go. See? I wasn't going to leave you lying there. What kind of aunt do you think I am?" She wrapped Rosie in a blanket and tuned into the voices coming from the living room. It was impossible to hear much of anything over Rosie's fussing.

Nerves had Peyton's stomach in knots as she left the bedroom. As soon she joined the guys, they both turned to look at her.

Jay motioned to his friend. "Peyton, this is Nate Walker, a good friend of mine. Nate, this is Peyton Kennedy."

There was a slight pause before he spoke her last name, but she doubted Nate would have caught it.

Nate was several inches taller than Jay, with dark hair

and expressive dark eyes. He stepped forward and held out a hand. "It's good to meet you."

"You, too." She shook it and forced a smile. "How do you two know each other?"

The guys exchanged a look before Nate responded. "It's a long story. Something I hear we might have in common."

For the first time, he looked at Rosie, who was waving her arms. After fussing and coughing, she was finally starting to calm down again.

Jay motioned for her to take the recliner. As soon as she did, he sat on one end of the couch and Nate on the other.

Peyton settled Rosie in her lap and began to rock. The baby immediately calmed, her wide brown eyes taking in the room.

There were several moments of silence punctuated by Rosie's coos and a slight squeak coming from the recliner.

Jay cleared his throat. "Peyton, Nate is a retired police detective. That's why I called him. He may be able to give us some advice or even find out some details that we might not be able to get otherwise."

She didn't like this at all. "And why wouldn't you feel obligated to call in and report my location?"

Nate leaned forward. "Because Jay is my friend. I trust him. And *he* trusts *you*." He shrugged as though that was the only answer she needed. He opened an electronic tablet and withdrew a stylus. "Why don't you start at the beginning?"

Trina's eyes, devoid of life, popped to mind. She squeezed her own closed against the image. She took in a steadying breath, sent up a silent prayer for strength, and began.

As she told them what happened, Nate furiously wrote down every detail while Jay made a note here and there in a notebook. It took everything in her to relay Trina's death. She hadn't realized tears were flowing until Jay stood, retrieved a box of tissues, and handed them to her with a gentle squeeze of her shoulder.

She nodded her thanks and took a moment to compose herself. Rosie tried to reach for the tissues, and Peyton moved them farther away.

She cleared her throat. "That's when I heard a second male voice. I ran back to the nursery and barricaded myself in the room as best I could."

Nate looked up from his notes. "Can you describe the voices? Anything could be helpful. Accents. An odd word either might have used."

Peyton closed her eyes and shivered as she replayed those few minutes in her mind.

"The first guy, the one that seemed to be arguing..." She willed the tears to stop flowing. "His voice was deep, like bass singer deep. No accent. Nothing I noticed, anyway. It didn't sound familiar. But there was something about the second guy. His voice was average in volume and tone. Slight southern accent, although that's probably true of half the people around here. But even still, there was something familiar about it. I can't quite place it, though."

"You don't have any idea where you might have heard it before?" The question came from Jay.

She shook her head. "There's no telling. Trina... She had a lot of men in her life. It was hard to keep track." Peyton hated speaking ill of her sister now that she was gone, but it was the truth. And right now, they needed to figure out what was going on and who might be behind all of this. "Then I see hundreds of people every day at my job, so who knows who all I've spoken to there."

If not showing up last night wasn't enough to get fired,

any connection to murder and kidnapping would certainly do it.

Nate made another set of notes on his tablet. "And your sister never mentioned that she expected someone to come by the house that night?"

"No."

The retired detective nodded for her to continue.

She told them about how she got them out of the house, snuck around, and ran to her car. "There was a strange car out front. I didn't recognize it, but I did take a picture of the license plate. I tried to give that information to the 9-1-1 dispatcher, but she only wanted me to turn myself in."

Nate's eyes widened. "So you've got the license plate for the car the killers drove in?"

"I'm pretty sure it belonged to them." She leaned forward to retrieve her phone from her back pocket. As soon as she had it in front of her, Rosie batted at it with her hands.

Jay, who had an impressed look on his face, stood and reached for Rosie, who kept trying to grab the phone. "I can hold her while you do that."

After handing the baby to Jay, she turned on the phone and went to her photos. Her pulse pounded in her ears. She ignored the other photos, touched the one she was looking for, and handed the phone to Nate.

He recited the license plate number and then turned the phone to show the picture to Jay.

He leaned closer. "Looks like a Chevy Equinox. Not sure of the year. Dark gray maybe?"

Peyton thought it was dark gray, too. She accepted the phone, turned it off, and set it on the coffee table.

"Great work." Nate gave a satisfied nod.

Jay gave Rosie a smile before focusing on Nate. "Is there

any way you can look that up? See who the car is registered to?"

"Me personally? Once I left the department, I lost access to that kind of software. But I know someone who could, and I'm certain he'll help us."

The nervous energy from before intensified. Peyton stood from the recliner and paced to the small fireplace on the far side of the living room. "I'm not sure that's a good idea. The more people who know about this, the higher the chance that someone is going to say something. I can't lose Rosie. I won't. Not after I've already lost Trina." Her voice broke.

She focused on the bricks that made up the fireplace. Their shapes. Shades. Anything to keep from picturing Trina's face again.

"You don't have to worry about Logan. He's IT at the Destiny Police Department. We go way back. He'll help us, almost no questions asked."

Peyton wanted to believe Nate. But she didn't know him. Certainly didn't know Logan. It'd been hard enough to come here to ask Jay for help.

She worried that someone was going to decide it was easier to report her to the police. If that happened, then she wouldn't be able to help Rosie. Protect her.

It wasn't just that, though. What if the guys who killed Trina wanted to silence Peyton, too? What if, by coming to Destiny, she was leading murderers right to Jay's doorstep?

Chapter Eight

Jay shifted Rosie to his shoulder. His palm nearly covered the baby's tiny back as he rubbed it in a calming circular motion. Most of his experience with babies revolved around his practice as a doctor. When his twin nephews were born, his brother and his family had already moved to New York. Jay held each of them maybe once or twice. The next time he saw them, they were active toddlers running around the room.

With his brother in New York and his parents in Chicago, they saw each other once a year at Christmas. It worked for their family, but right now, with Rosie in his arms, Jay realized how much they all missed by not being closer.

His attention swung to Peyton. She stood by the fireplace, her hands clasped in front of her. He couldn't see her face, but he'd bet she was worrying her bottom lip.

Nate had his phone to his ear. "Hey, I have a favor. Off the books." He lifted his tablet. "I need you to run a set of plates for me and let me know who the car is registered to."

He rattled off the number and then sat in silence with

his pen poised above the tablet. But when Logan must have come back with an answer, Nate set his tablet on the coffee table with a frown. "I appreciate it. Yes, I remember. Deep dish, double cheese, ham, pineapple, and olives. You've got it, man. Thanks again."

Peyton turned, her expression expectant.

"Unfortunately, the plates came back stolen." Nate gave her an apologetic look. "It does suggest more than a crime of passion, which lines up with what you said about them searching for something in the house."

She shook her head, her short hair brushing her cheeks. "What did you get yourself mixed up in, Trina?" The words were a whisper, but they echoed Jay's own thoughts.

Nate retrieved a laptop from the bag he'd brought in. "Jay mentioned that he couldn't find any reports about your sister's murder. I'm going to do some more searching and see if I can find anything. I may have a contact in Houston that I can reach out to as well." With that, his attention snapped to the screen.

Rosie sneezed. The baby's nose was so congested that it made Jay's heart hurt. "We're going to need a few things for Rosie. I'll get my computer, and we'll place an order. I have a membership and can get everything delivered here in a couple of hours." He handed the baby over.

He got his computer, set it up on the kitchen table, and was happy when Peyton joined him there. He scrolled through the website and added saline spray, a bulb syringe, liquid acetaminophen, a humidifier, and some baby shampoo to the cart. Then he did a search for Peyton's favorite shampoo. He knew she still used it because even now he could smell the faint scent of vanilla wafting from her hair. He added that to his cart and stood.

"Okay, now it's your turn. Add anything you need." He motioned to the computer and held his hands out for Rosie.

Peyton shook her head. "This is too much, Jay. I can't even pay you back right now. I don't know when I'll be able to."

Jay only took Rosie and put a hand on Peyton's back, ignoring the spark of awareness that surged at the touch. He urged her to take a seat. "You came to me for help. This is part of that. I can take a guess at some of the things you might need, but I don't think you want me to."

Her cheeks turned pink, and she started typing.

He'd volunteered to go to the store for her the first year of their marriage after her period had started. She'd needed some feminine products. He'd gone with the best of intentions but came back with all the wrong things, except for chocolate ice cream. At least he'd gotten something right.

It felt like a lifetime ago. He missed how they were back then. In love. Their whole future ahead of them. Realities of life hadn't set in yet.

He missed *her*.

Jay had done everything to get past their divorce. To move forward and figure out a life without her. He'd done that. He knew it was possible.

But that didn't mean it was what he wanted.

There were a lot of things he'd do differently if he could go back in time right now. So many things.

"Okay. That should be it." Peyton stood and took Rosie back. She touched his arm as her chin lifted, her eyes seeking his. "Thank you."

It took everything in him not to reach out and pull her into a hug. Instead, he only nodded and then sat down to complete the order. She'd chosen the absolute bare necessities, including a toothbrush and a hairbrush.

If Peyton and Rosie only stayed with him for a night or two, they would need everything in the order. Even more so if they decided to go somewhere else. The thought of Peyton in danger and him not being around to help her... to protect her. It was a situation Jay refused to consider right now, even though he knew the possibility of her leaving was high. She'd never been one to confront conflict head-on.

And he'd been the one who wanted to stand toe-to-toe with it. To fix everything, even if it was beyond his capabilities.

No wonder things fell apart between them.

"Hey, guys." Nate waved them in from the living room and gave Peyton an apologetic look. "There's nothing specific, but there *is* a small article online about a woman who was found dead from a fatal head wound. An investigation is underway, but they suspect a robbery gone wrong." He told them what part of town the home was in.

Peyton nodded numbly. "That's Trina's neighborhood."

Nate thought for a moment and swallowed hard. "I'm sorry for what you're going through, Peyton. I can imagine how much of a nightmare this has been..." His voice trailed off, and a haunted shadow passed his face.

Jay felt for his friend. They'd met in group therapy, and Nate had shared some of what brought him there. He'd been investigating a kidnapping case involving a child. A case that didn't have a happy ending. Nate blamed himself for the outcome, but Jay knew it'd been beyond his friend's control.

He prayed for Nate and then again for Peyton.

She reclaimed the recliner with Rosie, and Jay took the couch.

Nate cleared his throat. "If there's more to the case than

what was written in the article, then it's possible the police are doing their best to keep details close to the vest."

"Then they could consider Peyton a suspect, even if that information hasn't been made public." Jay frowned.

Nate closed his laptop and set it on the coffee table as though it had offended him. "I'd like to reach out to my buddy in Houston. See what I can find out. I'm not going to tell him your location, but with your permission, I'd like to let him know that I'm working a different angle." He looked to Peyton. "I'd simply ask for some extra details about the case. See if we can get any information that hasn't been made public. Are you okay with that?"

"This little circle of ours is getting bigger and bigger." She sighed and pressed her fingertips against her forehead as though willing herself to focus.

Jay leaned forward and tapped her arm. "We can't fight an enemy we know nothing about."

"Yeah." She focused on Nate. "Let's do it."

Nate gave her a definitive bob of his head. "I'm going to give him a call, and hopefully, he'll get back to me as soon as possible." He glanced at his watch. "In the meantime, I need to get home and let my dog out. If I don't do that soon, she'll be sure to leave me evidence of her displeasure." Nate gave a low chuckle and shoved everything back into the bag he'd brought with him. "I'll call as soon as I hear anything. Keep me in the loop, yeah?"

"We will." Jay stood and gave his friend a quick hug. "Appreciate the help, brother."

"Anytime. I'll be praying. Call if you need anything."

The last sentence was said in a hushed voice. If anyone knew how hard losing Peyton had been for Jay, it was Nate.

Jay walked his friend out. When he got back to the living room, he found Peyton rocking Rosie. The baby was wide awake, her fists waving in the air, but Peyton's eyes were closed. He might have thought she was asleep if it weren't for her feet moving to keep the chair going.

He knelt next to the chair and put a hand on her arm. "Why don't you let me look at that wound of yours? Then I'll keep an eye on Rosie for a while so you can go get some rest."

Her eyes opened, and she immediately shook her head. "I don't need to. I'm okay."

"You're clearly exhausted."

"And every time I start to fall asleep, I see it all over again. I see her lying there... all the blood..." Her jaw clenched, and her eyes filled with tears. "What if I'd gone out there right after Trina came home? Maybe I could have stopped everything from happening."

"Or maybe you'd be lying there on the floor alongside her."

Peyton didn't even try to wipe away the tears that raced down her cheeks.

He hated that there was nothing he could do to take away her pain. Or the memories of seeing her sister die right in front of her.

"Playing the what-if game is dangerous. Trust me. I've had to learn that the hard way." He'd struggled with that very problem for years. "There was nothing you could do for Trina. But you saved Rosie's life and your own. I only met your sister a couple of times, but I have no doubt that's what she would have wanted you to do."

She sniffed. "Yeah. She would have."

Jay reached for a tissue and handed it to her. "We're going to figure this out. You're not alone."

Chapter Nine

It was a good thing Peyton didn't try to take a nap because, thirty minutes later, the delivery order Jay made showed up early. While he was unpacking that and putting things away, Rosie needed to be changed and fed.

Peyton had to walk back and forth across the living room to calm her down. The poor baby would try to drink her bottle only to get angry because she could barely breathe through her nose. She'd stop to take a breath and cry. Over and over again.

"I hate this." It didn't matter how she tried to bounce or sway; it did nothing to temper Rosie's crying. Peyton's arm ached where she'd caught it on the window last night. She'd avoided having Jay look at it, but he was probably right. She should probably see how bad it was.

"There's not much worse than hearing a baby cry and being unable to do a thing about it." Jay looked up from where he was assembling the humidifier at the kitchen table. "We'll get this running, clear out her nose, and use some saline spray. That'll definitely help."

"I sure hope so." What would Trina be doing right now? Would Rosie be calmer if her mama were rocking her and tending to her?

It was up to Peyton now. The realities of what it would mean to raise Rosie hit her hard. How was she going to afford daycare?

She groaned.

"What's the matter?" Jay stopped filling the humidifier tank in the sink and turned the water off so he could hear her.

"I just realized I probably lost my job. There's no way my boss will let me keep it after no-showing last night."

Forget affording daycare. How was she going to pay her rent? Buy clothes, diapers, and formula?

The sudden responsibility of caring for Rosie and all that entailed felt like a boulder sitting right on the base of her neck.

"Surely, once everything gets figured out, your boss will realize it wasn't your fault." He turned the water back on and finished filling the tank. Once he had it fitted on the humidifier, he flipped the switch, and a moist cloud was pushed into the air.

"Not likely." When she realized he was watching her and waiting for her to elaborate, she continued. "I've been late for work a lot over the last few weeks. Trina... she wasn't always good about getting back to the house on time. I'm pretty sure my boss has been looking for an excuse to let me go."

"Where do you work?"

Suddenly, Peyton didn't want to share that information. When they were married, she had a secure job managing a local restaurant and then taught piano lessons on the weekends—most of them had been for friends, but it'd been a start. It'd been her hope to eventually teach full-time.

Where she worked in Houston? It was a huge step down.

She managed to get Rosie to latch on to the bottle again. The poor baby's eyes slid shut with relief as a single tear escaped.

She'd hoped Jay would forget he'd asked the question, but no such luck.

"Peyton? Where do you work?"

"I work nights stocking shelves at the grocery store down the street from where I live." She kept her gaze on Rosie.

When she finally glanced his way, he was busy in the kitchen. But his jaw was clenched, the muscle in his neck pulsing like it always did when he disapproved of something.

Her face heated with embarrassment. She shouldn't care what he thought about her. None of that mattered once they'd signed the divorce papers, right?

It was going to take more than that to convince herself.

The doorbell rang again. Jay glanced at his watch and checked to see who it was before opening the door.

"Hi, Erica," he greeted. "I didn't expect you to come by personally after speaking with Bryce."

"I was planning to make a trip by the church anyway, so it worked out well. I have a couple of boxes in my car. Do you mind helping me bring them in?"

"Not at all."

The two of them walked out, leaving the front door open. Moments later, they returned, each carrying a cardboard box full of clothing that they set on the kitchen table.

Jay shut the door and made introductions. "Erica, this is Peyton. Peyton, do you remember my friend, Bryce?"

"Of course." Jay and Bryce had been friends since before she and Jay ever met.

"Erica is his sister. We hadn't seen each other in a while, but we were both at Bryce and Megan's wedding."

"It's nice to meet you, Erica." She flashed the other woman a welcoming smile. "I didn't realize he'd gotten married. When did that happen?"

"This last November." Erica stepped forward and looked at Rosie with a smile. "She's beautiful. My son is ten now. It's hard to believe he was ever that tiny."

"This is my niece, Rosie. They do grow fast. I can't believe how much bigger she is now compared to when she was born."

The other woman smiled, her blue eyes kind. She pointed at the boxes behind her. "I brought some clothing for both you and the baby. Feel free to keep whatever fits or pass items along if they don't."

Peyton's eyes widened as she looked from the boxes to Jay and back at Erica. "Are you serious?"

Erica smiled kindly. "Absolutely. It's a ministry that my church feels strongly about, as do I. I hope the clothing blesses you. And whatever challenge you're facing now, I pray for peace, strength, and a resolution."

"Thank you. Truly." Peyton's eyes stung with unshed tears. "Is it okay if I... Can I give you a hug?"

"Of course!" She stepped forward and wrapped her arms gently around Peyton and Rosie. When she stepped back, she gave them a smile. "If you need anything else, please call me. I'm sorry I have to run. School is letting out early today, and I need to pick up my son. Take care of yourselves."

She turned to Jay. "It was good to see you."

"You, too, Erica. Thanks again."

While Jay walked her to the front door, Peyton approached the boxes of clothing in awe. One was filled with everything Rosie could possibly need.

And the other? Peyton couldn't wait to change out of what she was wearing now. She was sweaty and bloody and felt like an absolute mess. It would be a huge blessing to be able to change into some fresh clothing.

Jay walked up behind her. "Erica and her group at the Nazarene church are some of the sweetest people."

Peyton nodded, not trusting herself to speak.

"Let's see if Rosie will be content in the crib for a few minutes so I can take a look at your arm. Then I'll rock her while you take a shower and change."

"Yeah. That would be great." She couldn't wait to wash away the sweat and grime.

"I'll go grab the first aid kit."

She looked at the clothing boxes again, and a tiny purple dress caught her eye. She reached into the box and pulled it out. It was the very same dress that Trina had bought for Rosie not even a week ago.

She ran her thumb over the fabric. The tears she'd kept at bay moments ago broke through, and she sniffed. Too bad a shower couldn't rid her of all that had happened last night.

A door closing in the other room shook Peyton from her thoughts. She put the dress back, swiped away the tears, and went into the guest room. Once she got Rosie settled with a rattle in the portable crib, she found Jay waiting for her in the hallway.

"Let's go in the bathroom. The lighting is better." He followed her in.

Peyton spotted her reflection in the mirror and

grimaced. The eyes that stared back at her had dark circles under them and were red-rimmed from crying.

The blood on her shirt was her own, but it immediately took her back to the house, and a shiver ran down her spine. She closed her eyes for a moment and drew in a deep breath.

When she opened them again, she found Jay watching her. She knew that look. Worry, with a hint of appreciation and determination.

She broke eye contact, unwilling to examine her own emotions right now. Instead, she tried to pull the sleeve of her shirt up over her wound but hissed in pain.

"I've got a tank top under this, and the shirt needs to be trashed anyway."

She always wore tank tops just in case she had to change shirts in the parking lot of the grocery store before going to work. It'd happened more than once when Trina got home too late for Peyton to get home and change.

She cringed at the memory and carefully lifted the T-shirt over her head. Her shoulder protested, and she bit her lip to keep from crying out.

Jay let out a low whistle. "Honey, we should've cleaned this up hours ago."

His use of the word "honey" caught her by surprise, but he didn't seem to realize he'd used it.

"If it were on your face or somewhere visible, I'd suggest stitches." His gaze lifted, and he looked at her. Immediately, his expression softened. "I think butterfly bandages will be just fine here. Why don't you take a shower first, and then I'll clean it up and put some antibiotic cream on there before we cover it?"

She nodded her agreement and tried to ignore the way his touch warmed her skin. When they were together, there'd been nowhere more comforting than to be wrapped in his arms. They disagreed about a lot, especially after he came back from his last tour in Afghanistan. Sometimes, it seemed like all they did was argue.

Until they held each other. Whether it was cuddling on the couch watching TV, walking hand-in-hand, or during more intimate moments, she always felt cherished. Loved.

Oh, how she missed that. Missed him. Her heart ached with longing. If only they could go back to what they had. Or what they could have had.

His phone rang. His hands dropped from her arm when he answered it. "This is Jay." He caught her eyes in the mirror and mouthed, "Nate."

Jay lightly brushed her arm with his hand and stepped away.

Peyton swept the trash from the counter into her hand and deposited it into the wastebasket, then followed him into the hallway.

"Yeah, that would be great." He glanced at his watch. "We'll see you then. Of course, I don't mind a bit. Yep. Bye." He hung up and slid his phone back into his pocket. "Nate's contact in Houston texted him back. They have a virtual meeting scheduled for late this afternoon. He said he'll be by the house again around five to share what he knows."

Chapter Ten

Jay held Rosie in his arms as he passed the bathroom. The clean scent of vanilla seeped beneath the door and filled the hallway. The familiar smell brought back memories of the bubble baths Peyton always loved to take. He pictured her in the bathtub now, surrounded by bubbles, and his chest hurt. When they were married, he would sometimes go in and kiss her. She would reach up and grasp his shirt to pull him down for a second kiss. He'd walk away with a wet shirt and a full heart. Worth it every single time.

Was she remembering their kisses now, too? Or was it all part of the distant past for her? Did being here with him affect her at all?

He wished he knew.

Then again, maybe he didn't want to know. That seemed like a recipe for disaster, no matter how he looked at it.

With a frustrated puff of air, he carried Rosie into the living room. He focused on her as he suctioned her nose, gave her some saline spray, and held her at the table near the humidifier. She still had a low-grade fever, but that wasn't necessarily a bad thing. It meant her body was fighting off whatever virus was plaguing her. Hopefully, the little one would be feeling better in another day or two.

Rosie relaxed in his arms as he cradled her. The baby's dark eyes focused on his face until her eyelids began to get heavy. He carefully carried her to the recliner, where he started rocking softly. It wasn't long before she was fast asleep on his chest.

Jay considered taking her to the crib but couldn't quite make himself. There was something about holding her close that was comforting. When she gave a little sigh of peace, his heart melted.

His attention drifted to the piano. He'd noticed Peyton looking at it earlier. He tried to sell it more than once after the divorce, but he never could make himself. The piano itself was beautiful, with dark wood and a matching bench. It certainly added character to the living room.

But truthfully, he hadn't been able to sell it because it reminded him of better times. Of a house filled with music. He loved coming home to hear the notes filtering through the front door and welcoming him in.

He'd told himself that maybe he'd learn to play one day. But if Jay were honest with himself, a part of him hoped she might come back and ask if she could have the piano after all.

It'd been foolish.

The bathroom door opened, and a billow of steam poured into the hallway. A few minutes later, Peyton walked into the room and stopped just behind the recliner. He couldn't see her, but her scent enveloped him, and the chair rocked slightly as though she'd placed a hand on the back.

"She fell asleep about ten minutes ago."

"That's good. Sweet baby is exhausted." Peyton rounded the chair and sat down on the couch.

Her damp hair hung just long enough to brush her shoulders. She'd found a pair of dark jeans to wear along with a long, flowing shirt that looked as though it had been made for her. The hints of green in the fabric brought out the matching color in her eyes.

"Do you feel better?"

"Much." She watched Rosie for several moments before raising her gaze. "Yesterday feels like a different lifetime."

"I can only imagine."

The baby wasn't the only exhausted person in the room.

"Why don't I put Rosie down, we patch up your arm, and then see if you can get some rest before Nate comes back?"

It looked like she was going to object, but he suspected her body was nearly at its limit.

Finally, she gave him a small nod.

Rosie barely moved as he got her settled. Peyton was waiting for him in the bathroom, the first aid kit lying open on the counter.

Since the shirt she was wearing was short-sleeved, it was easier to get to the wound. He gently rolled the sleeve up, cleaned it, and then applied a layer of antibiotic cream. Carefully, he put two butterfly bandages in place to keep it closed.

Peyton watched him in the mirror as he worked. The man was handsome, always had been, but the goatee made him look even more so. She had the sudden urge to run her hand over the bristles to see what it felt like. Before she did something stupid, she dragged her attention away from him and focused on her arm.

Jay covered the area with a large bandage to keep out the dirt and germs. He shook two acetaminophen tablets from a bottle and gave them to her. "Let me know if your the area gets warm or hurts more, okay? I'll go get you some water."

When he'd returned, she was in the guest room sitting on the bed. She accepted the bottle, swallowed the medication, and set it down on the side table. "You'll wake me up when Nate gets here?"

"I will. Get some rest."

She nodded once, and he left the room, leaving the door open a crack behind him. He said a silent prayer that she'd be able to sleep.

He spent the majority of the following two hours checking for new articles about Trina's death but found nothing that Nate hadn't already shared.

Next, he tried to find what he could about Trina herself.

She had a Facebook account, and while Jay couldn't see who her friends were, most of her posts were public. He scrolled through them and counted at least three that talked about starting a new job in the last year. Peyton mentioned that Trina worked at a restaurant. According to the public posts, she'd only been working there for the last five months or so.

Her birthdate wasn't listed on her About page, but it did say she was in a relationship with a man called Stephen Lewis. He jotted the information down.

Peyton had mentioned the situation between Trina and Rosie's father was a long story. He thought this evening might be a good time to elaborate on that.

Without any idea what Trina's killers were after or why, as far as Jay was concerned, everyone was a suspect.

Did Trina realize she'd gotten herself into something

that would eventually endanger her family? Or had she been completely taken by surprise when the two men showed up at her house?

Jay had only met Trina twice. She'd stood as Peyton's maid of honor at their wedding, and she hadn't stayed for long after the ceremony. He knew Trina visited Peyton several times while he was deployed.

When he'd asked Peyton about it, she assured him that Trina didn't have anything against him. He couldn't imagine why she refused to come around while he was there otherwise.

Trina hadn't left a good impression.

He didn't like to think ill of the dead, but he'd be lying if he didn't admit he was considering the possibility that Trina had been into something that brought trouble right to Peyton's door. And, consequently, his as well.

Out of curiosity, he did a search for Peyton on Facebook.

Her account was set to private, and it looked like she only had about twenty friends, although specifics weren't available. He wondered who was on the list. Unlike her sister, there were no public posts. Even her profile picture was of a cartoon character instead of a personal photo.

Jay's phone pinged with a text from Nate.

"I promised Logan a pizza. Figured I'd pick one up for us too. What does Peyton like?"

His friend's thoughtfulness reinforced Jay's decision to include him in the situation.

"Pepperoni."

"Easy enough. Be there in twenty."

He closed that internet tab and turned to his notes. He reviewed everything Peyton had told them earlier.

Some minutes later, he stood and made his way back to

the guest room. Peyton had said to wake her up when Nate got there, but he knew she'd appreciate a few minutes to recover from the nap before his friend arrived.

He found her lying on her side, one arm curled around a pillow. Some of her hair rested against her cheek. A quick peek into the crib assured him that Rosie was still asleep, although probably not for much longer.

He gently touched Peyton's shoulder. "Hey. It's time to wake up. Nate will be here anytime now."

When she opened her eyes, she squinted in confusion for a heartbeat or two before focusing on him. "Yeah. Thanks." She sat up and ran a hand down her face. "How long was I out?"

"Over two hours."

Her brows rose, and she checked the clock as though she didn't believe him. "Wow." She glanced at Rosie. "I guess we were both more tired than I realized."

Jay wasn't the least bit surprised, but he didn't say anything. Instead, he pointed his thumb toward the door behind him. "I'll go so you can take your time. Just come on out when you're ready. No rush."

She nodded her understanding, and he left.

He'd barely made it to the living room when the doorbell rang. He found Nate outside with his messenger bag hanging over one shoulder, two pizza boxes in his hands, and his Rottweiler standing beside him.

"Come on in." Jay took the boxes from him and set them on the kitchen table. Nate's dog, Minnie, had followed him. He reached down and gave her ear a scratch.

Nate shut the door behind him. "Sorry it took a little longer than I thought. I ran a pizza by the station for Logan. Something tells me we're going to need his help again before all of this is over."

"Good thinking."

Logan Alcott's love of Hawaiian pizza with black olives was well-known. Just the thought of pineapple on pizza was nearly enough to ruin Jay's appetite.

On the other hand, the tantalizing scents of pepperoni and sausage that wafted from the boxes led him to retrieve plates from a cabinet in the kitchen. "I appreciate you bringing dinner by."

"Not a problem." Nate scanned the room. "How's Peyton doing?"

"She's hanging in there. She and the baby both got some sleep, which is good."

Nate helped himself to a can of soda from the fridge. He turned and studied Jay. "What about you? How are *you* doing?"

"It's complicated," he said as Peyton walked into the room.

She'd brushed her hair, and it curled in slightly next to her chin. Her eyes lit up when she saw the pizza boxes.

Nate tossed Jay a look that promised a longer conversation later.

Minnie started to approach her, but Nate snapped his fingers. "Sit."

The dog obeyed immediately.

Peyton looked impressed. "Boy or girl?"

"Girl. Her name's Minnie."

Peyton didn't look like she believed him, and Jay chuckled. Whenever the dog was introduced, it was always interesting to watch the person try to reconcile the name with the size of the animal.

"She's beautiful. Is she full Rottweiler?" Peyton took several steps closer, a soft expression on her face.

"Yes. At least as far as I know."

"May I pet her?"

"Sure." Nate snapped his fingers again. "Okay, Minnie."

The dog stood to her feet, her nub of a tail wagging back and forth as Peyton held out a hand for her to sniff. Within moments, she was scratching both ears while Minnie leaned against her legs, a look of bliss on her face.

Nate moved to stand next to Jay and lowered his voice. "Complicated, huh?"

"Oh, yeah."

There was too much at stake. Jay needed to focus on figuring out who killed Trina and whether they were after Peyton or not. He would deal with the mess of everything else later.

Chapter Eleven

The pepperoni pizza tasted heavenly, and Peyton even made it through her second slice before Rosie woke up. Jay, who'd eaten much faster than she, volunteered to get the baby and even made her a bottle using a canister of formula he'd brought from the clinic.

He sat back down at the table, looking completely natural with Rosie drinking hungrily in his arms.

If things had gone differently, and they hadn't gotten a divorce, where would they be now? Would he be rocking a child of their own? The thought made her frown, and she consciously shoved it away.

Going down that path was pointless because it didn't matter. They were here now, and what was done was done.

Besides, it wouldn't be long before she'd be leaving again, and it would be up to her to care for and raise Rosie. Alone.

It wasn't fair that Trina wouldn't get to watch her daughter celebrate her first birthday, graduate from kinder-garten, or go to her first dance. It wasn't right that Rosie wouldn't even remember her mother.

Peyton jumped when a hand touched hers. She looked up, not realizing she'd been staring at her plate, to find both Jay and Nate watching her with concern.

Her cheeks heated. The last thing she needed to do was fall apart again.

She focused on Nate. "Were you able to learn anything from your contact in Houston?"

The ex-detective cleaned his hands off on a paper towel, pushed his plate away, and reached for his bag. "Lee Patterson. Yes, he's a detective in Houston, although he works in a different precinct than the one in the area where your sister lived. He was able to verify that the body that was found was your sister's. He's reached out to the person in charge of the case, Detective Abbott, and is hoping for more information. Usually, there's some degree of cooperation between officers and detectives, but Abbott is keeping everything quiet."

Peyton took another bite of her pizza and then pushed the plate away. "Meaning what?"

Nate opened his laptop. "It could simply mean that Abbott has no information about the case at this time, and it's still early in the investigation. Or it could be a sign of something significant. That details are being buried. I'm more inclined to go with the latter."

The baby finished her bottle, and Jay lifted her to his shoulder and gently patted her back. "Was Detective Patterson able to determine whether Peyton was still a suspect or not?"

"Abbott was very tight-lipped. However, Patterson used to work with several people at Abbott's precinct. Since going directly to Abbott didn't work, he's going to reach out to those individuals instead. But it may take a day or two to get any information. Meanwhile, he's going to do some investigating on his own. He promised to call me as soon as he hears anything."

Rosie gave a hearty burp, eliciting chuckles all around the table.

Peyton reached for the baby, and Jay handed her over.

He looked at his notebook and hesitated. Finally, he looked up. "Peyton? I know you couldn't hear much of the conversation, but did it sound like Trina knew the two men?"

The smile that had been on her face as she interacted with Rosie faded instantly. She looked past him to the window in the small dining room. Her heart ached.

Her gaze shifted to him again. "She knew at least one of them. I recognized one of the voices, too, but I can't place it. I wish I could."

"It's okay. Maybe it'll come to you later." Jay tapped his pen against his notepad. "Why don't you tell us about Rosie's father and any of the men that have been in Trina's life recently."

Nate nodded. "Once we get names, I can call Logan and have him run some background checks. See if anything sends up a red flag or if anyone's suddenly gone on vacation."

Rosie sneezed and then gave an adorable coo as she batted at Peyton's watch.

Peyton ran a hand over the baby's soft hair and a thumb across her chubby little cheek. She kept her focus on her niece as she began. "Rosie's father's name is Jeb Carter. He and Trina only dated for a few months. As soon as he found out Trina was pregnant, he accused her of sleeping around and insisted the baby wasn't his. He hasn't been around much since."

She couldn't imagine leaving her own child behind like

that. "Trina was better off. They both were. Jeb was a loose cannon. He was into some bad things. I know drugs were involved, but I don't think that was the worst of it. He never laid a hand on Trina as far as I know, but there were times I think he would have if I hadn't been there."

Nate frowned, the disgust evident on his face. "Did you ever have any doubt that Jeb was the father?"

Peyton shook her head. "None. Trina... There were a lot of men. She's never known what to do on her own and refuses to try. But she wasn't a cheater. She said Jeb was Rosie's father, and I have no reason to think otherwise."

A flash of sympathy passed over Jay's face. "Did Jeb ever see Rosie?"

"Not that I know of. Trina went to him two different times when she was desperate for money. He gave her some. The second time, he told her not to bother him again. It wasn't long after that before she got involved with Stephen Lewis. Her most recent boyfriend." Who wasn't much better, as far as Peyton was concerned.

Then again, she couldn't recall a single boyfriend that Trina introduced her to that Peyton could say she genuinely liked.

Jay looked thoughtful. "Is there any chance the money had been a loan? One that he had hoped to get back by now?"

"Trina never referred to the money as loans. To be fair, I'm not sure she would have told me even if they were." There were a lot of things they didn't talk about.

Nate wrote something down. "We'll look into Jeb, especially from the loan angle. Okay, tell us about Stephen."

Peyton shrugged. "He rarely came to Trina's house while I was there. I only met him twice, and both times, I had gone over to watch Rosie so they could go out on a date.

He barely said a word to me." She'd never cared for the man, and she'd never been convinced that he truly cared about Trina either. She told the guys that. "I got the impression that he resented the time Trina spent with Rosie and even the hours she worked at the restaurant."

Nate was busy writing everything down. "Where did he work?"

"I have no idea. Trina never said."

"Sounds like we need to figure that out." Jay looked like he wanted to say something but was wrestling with whether he should. Finally, he spoke again. "Are you certain neither of the men there last night were Jeb or Stephen?"

"Without a doubt. It wasn't either of them." Their voices seemed to echo in her head, and then the tone of Trina's voice right before she died made Peyton's heart stall. She only half listened as the guys continued the conversation.

"But it doesn't mean there isn't a connection between the intruders and Jeb or Stephen." Jay stared at his notes. "At this point, we don't know why Trina was targeted or what they were truly after."

Nate nodded his agreement. "Agreed. I think—" His phone rang, and he swiped immediately to answer it. "Hey, Lee. I didn't expect to hear from you so soon." He glanced at Peyton. "Yep. I'll be watching for them. Thanks, man."

He ended the call and frowned. "Patterson went by your apartment, and a neighbor said that someone had been lurking around earlier in the day. He spoke to your landlord and expressed his concern. She let him into your place. Someone had already been inside, and they tore it apart."

Peyton tried to digest his words, but it wasn't until Nate handed her his phone and she started to scroll through the photos that the truth of them really hit home.

Her apartment was barely recognizable. Most of her belongings had been knocked over, strewn about, or destroyed. From the looks of the pictures, the destruction was consistent throughout the small space. She numbly handed the phone back.

She was barely aware of Nate passing the device to Jay for him to look at the pictures.

Rosie wiggled in her arms, and Peyton shifted her to her shoulder. She hadn't had a chance to even think about what life was going to look like going forward. She couldn't go back to Trina's house, and now she wondered if there would even be anything worth salvaging at her own.

A tell-tale smell drifted to her nose. She welcomed a reason to distract herself and stood. "I need to change Rosie."

She held the baby close as she made her way to the guest room.

What was she going to do? How was she going to take care of Rosie and give her everything she deserved if Peyton didn't even have a home to go back to?

Chapter Twelve

Peyton crept down the hallway as the voices filtered from the front of the house. She reached out to touch the walls, vaguely aware of the fact that they seemed faded as though they weren't quite in focus.

A scream pierced the air, and Trina's body dropped at Peyton's feet. She stared in horror as Trina reached toward her and whispered, "Save my baby."

Peyton's heart nearly beat out of her chest as she turned and ran back to the nursery. She locked the door, shoved the changing table in front of it, and then rushed to the crib.

Empty.

A bottle full of milk rested on the mattress, but there was no sign of Rosie.

"No!" A sob caught in Peyton's throat as she frantically searched the rest of the room.

A tapping on the window drew her around. She gasped.

A man stood just outside, his face out of focus and not recognizable. In his arms was Rosie. Without a word, the man turned and walked away.

"Rosie!"

The sound of Peyton's scream launched Jay from his bed. He slipped on his glasses. Then he pressed his thumb to the safe on his nightstand and took out his 9mm handgun. Gripping it, he flipped the hallway light on and rushed to the guest room.

He'd half expected to find an intruder lurking. Instead, Peyton was still asleep on the bed, but she looked anything but peaceful. Her face glimmered with tears, and she clutched a pillow to her as though she were afraid it was going to be ripped from her at any moment.

"No," she moaned, and the pain in her voice made Jay's heart twist.

"Peyton?" He rested a hand on her arm. "Honey, you're having a bad dream."

She sat upright and blinked at him with a shake of her head. "I can't find Rosie. He took her." With a shaky breath, she swiped at the tears.

Without another word, she stood and went to the crib where Rosie was fussing. The moment she saw the baby, her shoulders relaxed. "Thank God."

Jay watched as Peyton gently patted Rosie's diapered bottom. Gradually, the baby quieted and must have drifted back to sleep.

Peyton turned slowly. "I don't know what I would have done if I'd lost them both..."

The pain in her eyes drove Jay forward. He set his gun on the top of the dresser and wrapped his arms around her, pulling her close. Only then did he realize he wasn't wearing a shirt. He rarely did when he went to bed. After hearing Peyton scream, it was the last thing he'd been worried about.

76

If she minded, she didn't show it. Her hands were like ice on his back, her damp cheek pressed against his chest.

Jay breathed in her scent and savored the feel of her in his arms. He'd loved holding his wife. There were a lot of things he missed once they got divorced—too many things to count. But this closeness ranked among the top.

It took everything he had to take a step back and put a little space between them. He wasn't sure what time it was, but it was clear Peyton wouldn't be able to go back to sleep for a while. "Come on. Let's go make some hot chocolate."

It might have been September, but if there was one thing Peyton could never turn down, it was chocolate in any form and at any time.

She glanced at the crib again. Finally, she nodded.

He dropped his arms and ignored how much he already missed her. "I'm going to grab a shirt. I'll be right there."

In the kitchen, the microwave clock announced that it was almost three in the morning. In comfortable silence, he got two mugs from a cabinet and found the cocoa powder. She began to put the cocoa in the mugs while he heated up the milk. In no time, they were sitting at the kitchen table, each of them with their hot drink.

Peyton took a sip and gave an audible sigh. "Exactly what I needed. Thank you."

"No problem." He sipped at his own. It did hit the spot.

After a few moments, she tilted her head toward the canister of cocoa still sitting on the counter. "I'm surprised you had any on hand. It wasn't usually your beverage of choice."

He shrugged. But the look she gave him let him know that the wordless response wouldn't be enough.

Jay set his mug down. "It reminds me of you." He didn't drink it often, but occasionally, when he was missing what they used to have or watching a show they once enjoyed together, he'd make a cup.

Her eyebrows rose in surprise. She absently ran a thumb along the handle of her mug. "I keep cashews in my pantry. For the same reason."

Now, it was his turn to be shocked. She'd always hated cashews. Never ate them if she could help it. On the other hand, they were one of his favorite nuts, and he snacked on them frequently. "You ever eat them?"

"Sometimes. They aren't half bad."

He might have missed the slight upward curve at the corners of her mouth if he hadn't been watching her. "I never thought I'd see the day."

They both chuckled.

Silence returned, and so did the sad frown on Peyton's face.

Jay knew what it was like to be plagued with memories of something horrible, even when he finally relaxed enough to go to sleep. He truly felt for her. "The dreams. You'll keep having them for a while, but it will get better eventually."

"Sounds like you speak from experience." She held her mug in front of her like a shield. "After Afghanistan?"

He nodded.

She took a sip of her cocoa. "I knew you were having trouble sleeping. You never wanted to talk about it."

"No, I didn't. And that was a mistake." He'd shut a lot of people out back then, but especially Peyton. They'd been struggling for a while anyway, and the last thing he wanted to do was to appear weak in front of her. "About six months after the divorce, I started going to group therapy for people who have been through some kind of trauma." He used his thumbnail to scratch at an invisible spot on the table. "My deployment, not the divorce. Although both would qualify."

Peyton set her mug down, the hot chocolate forgotten. "I had no idea. Good for you, Jay."

He shrugged. "That's where I met Nate and several other guys I keep in touch with. We were all there for different reasons, but the need to forgive ourselves and move forward was something we shared. Still do."

Sometimes, he still had to forgive himself daily, but not nearly like he did back in the beginning. Back when it felt like the guilt would overwhelm him with every breath.

"I can't begin to compare my situation after the divorce to yours," Peyton began, "but when I moved to Houston and realized how much help Trina needed, I felt overwhelmed. How was I supposed to help her unravel her mess of a life when I couldn't even see my way out of mine?"

He nodded for her to continue.

"I started going to the church around the corner from where I lived at the time. They had a grief counseling class. I was having a hard time adjusting after the divorce but always figured grief counseling was for people who had lost loved ones to death." She swallowed, her eyes filling with tears. No doubt thinking about losing Trina now. "But the pastor's wife assured me it was for anyone, no matter how we lost someone in our lives."

She met his gaze and held it before looking away again.

"And did it help?"

"It did. Not just when it came to the divorce but even losing my parents at eighteen. I felt like I was losing Trina, too—to her bad decisions and lifestyle. I tried to get her to go to church with me, but she always made fun of it."

"I hope you didn't let it stop you."

She shook her head. "I was tired of running away from everything."

Her words settled over his heart. It was something he'd accused her of many times during their marriage and divorce.

Just like she'd always challenged him about his need to control and fix everything.

They'd both been right about the other's weaknesses, but neither was willing to acknowledge their own.

"I'm proud of you, Peyton."

"Thanks. I'm proud of you, too." She gave him a small smile. "I became a Christian early last spring. I've still got a lot to learn. But I can't imagine going through all of this... after Trina..." Her voice broke. "I'm thankful I have God in my life now."

Jay swallowed past a lump in his throat. "I became a Christian last spring, too." The timing of it all sent goose-bumps across his arms. "A few months into group therapy, Nate invited me to visit his church. I'll be honest. He practically had to drag me along by the ear. But I'm glad he did."

"I'm glad he did, too." She rubbed her arms with her hands as though she'd caught a chill.

Jay caught sight of her tiny heart tattoo and reached for her hand. He turned it over, exposing the ink. "I have to admit, I thought getting a tattoo was one of the last things you'd ever do." He released her hand.

"Yeah. Me, too." She ran a finger across the heart. "I got it after I became a Christian. Things were still hard, and I struggled a lot. I wanted a visual and permanent reminder that God was there for me no matter what I was going through."

"I think that was a beautiful idea."

She gave him a subtle tilt of her head in thanks before

picking up her mug and draining the last of the hot chocolate. It'd probably become cool by now, but she didn't seem to care. "I think I'm going to try and get some more sleep. I doubt it'll be much longer before Rosie wakes up. She seems to be resting well tonight. Maybe that means she's finally starting to feel better."

"I hope so." He stood from the table when she did. "I'll take care of the mugs. Sleep well. I'll be praying it'll be peaceful."

"Thank you."

She left the room, and he quietly gathered the mugs and set them in the sink before running water in them. He could wash them tomorrow. When he was done, Jay leaned against the kitchen counter, his hands gripping the edge on either side of him.

"Father God, thank You for keeping Peyton and Rosie safe and for bringing them here. Help them both to get some peaceful sleep that they desperately need. Please guide us as we try to get to the bottom of what happened to Trina. Give everyone involved the wisdom to see a solution."

He wanted to pray that God would find a way to keep Peyton in his life in some capacity after everything was sorted out, but it seemed like such a selfish request. If Peyton had a church home back in Houston, she may have plenty of friends willing to help her and Rosie. Houston was her home now. It was where her sister lived. Of course, Peyton would want to go back once she was safe to do so.

Jay didn't know what the future held, but he sure didn't like the idea of going back to not speaking or knowing what was going on in Peyton's life once all of this was over.

Chapter Thirteen

Everything around Peyton faded as she tried to make sense of what she'd just heard. It was barely nine o'clock in the morning. Nate had come by with a box of donuts and news from his contact, Detective Patterson, in Houston. Jay and Nate were talking, the clock above the mantel still ticking away the seconds, and yet it'd all gone to a low hum.

Trina's boyfriend, Stephen Lewis, was dead.

First Trina, and now this. It wasn't a coincidence.

A big part of Peyton had half hoped that, once she got out of Houston and the police had a chance to investigate everything surrounding Trina's murder, they would get things sorted out. That Peyton would find out she was cleared of any wrongdoing, the killers would be thrown in prison, and she could go back. Try to figure out what life is going to be like now.

Talk about naïve.

This wasn't over. Far from it.

"Peyton?"

Jay's voice startled her, and she jumped. Thankfully,

Rosie was taking a nap in the other room. Otherwise, it surely would have scared her, too.

She looked at his face and then Nate's. Apparently, they'd been speaking to her directly, then realized she wasn't hearing a thing.

"I'm sorry. What were you saying?"

The men exchanged concerned glances.

They were probably afraid to say too much. She got that, especially when she zoned out like she had. But as much as she didn't want to have this conversation or face what was happening, she refused to hide. She couldn't. Not when Trina's killers were still out there somewhere.

She straightened her spine and lifted her chin. "I'm okay."

Nate cleared his throat. "Stephen was found bound to a chair. He'd been beaten, but it was a single gunshot to the chest that killed him. Patterson said that ballistics is going to run the bullet through the system and compare it to the one that killed Trina. See if it's a match."

Peyton shoved the mental image of a beaten Stephen from her mind. She fully expected the bullets to match. The guy at Trina's house had sounded confident. Capable. A mental image of a bulldog came to mind, and she shivered. "I wish we knew what Stephen said. If anything."

"I know that Stephen and Trina were dating." Jay leaned forward and placed his arms on his knees. "Could she have told him anything about you? That you lived here before you moved to Houston? That we were married?"

She shrugged as frustration built. "I wish I knew. I have no idea what kind of relationship they had. She didn't like to talk about him. I think she was afraid I'd judge her or suggest she leave him." She frowned. "I probably would have, too. Any guy who didn't want to go to the house or get to know Rosie...that sent up big red flags in my book."

From the guys' expressions, it was clear they agreed with her.

Nate reached over and chose a glazed donut. "I think it's safe to assume they didn't find what they were looking for at Trina's house or at your apartment, Peyton."

Was it horrible to hope they'd gotten what they wanted from Stephen? Peyton cringed, and guilt immediately swept through her. Not that she'd wanted the man dead. But if they had gotten what they were searching for, then maybe she and Rosie were safe.

Even if that were true, she'd never know for sure. Would always wonder. Always be looking over her shoulder.

She had never been super close to Trina, but she wished she could talk to her right now. Call her up on the phone and...

Peyton stalled. Trina's phone. She'd forgotten all about it. "I'll be right back."

Without explanation, she ran into the guest room and dug through the diaper bag until she found the device. When she returned to the kitchen, both guys were waiting, concern and curiosity written on their faces.

She held the phone out to Nate. "It's Trina's. I forgot all about it. I think she'd been holding it when she was..." Peyton swallowed hard. "It landed by my foot in the hall-way. I grabbed it and ran to the nursery..." She swallowed again, but the lump remained in her throat. "She keeps it on silent at work."

If someone had tried to contact her, Peyton wouldn't have heard. She handed the phone to Jay, who passed it to Nate.

Nate examined the phone. "This is great. I'll take it to Logan and see what he can get from it. If there's a passcode, do you happen to know what it might be?"

"Not for sure. You could try Trina's birth year." She recited it for him, and he wrote it down. "Or Rosie's birthday. 0605 for June fifth." She hoped one of those was it. But if the police investigation shows she'd watched on television were even partially right, she guessed Logan would be able to get into the phone regardless.

Nate slipped the phone into his bag and finished his donut in a single bite. "I'm going to take this by Logan. I'll be in touch as soon as I hear something."

Jay tried to get him to take the rest of the donuts, but he refused. Minutes later, Jay was locking the front door again. He swiveled to face Peyton.

"Are you okay?" As soon as the words were out of his mouth, he scowled. "Dumb question."

She shrugged. "I don't even know right now." She prayed Trina's phone might give them a clue. Wait! The phone—she sat up straight as panic caused her chest to tighten. "Can you text Nate? Tell him I need that phone back once Logan is done with it. The pictures they..." Her voice cracked. If there were any pictures of Trina on there, she wanted them back. Needed them.

"Of course." Jay immediately sent a text before reclaiming his seat at the kitchen table. A ping announced an incoming text. He read it and gave a satisfactory nod. "Nate says he'll make sure you get it back as soon as possible."

"Thank you." Peyton reached for a donut and set it on the paper plate in front of her, but didn't pick it up again. "I wish we knew what they were looking for. Trina was a lot of things, but overly mysterious wasn't one of them. I'm having a hard time picturing her with some huge secret that she's kept hidden from me for the last two years."

Even as she said the words, she knew they weren't entirely true. She and Trina had never been good friends. Sisters, of course. Obviously, Trina trusted her enough to care for Rosie, which was nothing to sneeze at. But friends who confided in each other? Nope.

Would it surprise her to find that Trina had been hiding something all this time?

Not even a little.

Chapter Fourteen

Peyton seemed to be deep in thought as she stared at the chocolate-frosted donut in front of her. She still hadn't eaten anything, and Jay was trying to bite his tongue. The last thing she needed was for someone to start bossing her around. At least, that's how he was afraid she would see it. Truthfully, he was simply concerned for her health, both physical and mental.

If he weren't worried about someone potentially looking for her, he'd be tempted to take her to church tomorrow. It would be good for both of them.

As it was, though, it would be better if she and Rosie stayed out of sight.

He watched as she pinched a piece of the doughnut off and placed it on her tongue. Her attention wavered, her gaze shifting to the living room. A moment later, she looked back at him.

"You kept the piano."

A statement. Not a question. Yet she was watching him as though she expected some kind of response.

Jay shrugged. "The piano was too nice to just stick in a garage sale or something."

Disbelief flashed in her eyes. Yeah, he wouldn't have believed him, either. It was a small lie, but guilt pricked at him nonetheless.

He cleared his throat. "You loved that piano. I couldn't believe it when you said you didn't want it. I always thought you'd come back for it one day."

Peyton's eyes widened at his admission. "I had no idea. I figured you'd sell it the moment I left town."

She nibbled on her lower lip, and he hated that his first impulse was to reach across the table and touch her mouth.

As though she sensed what he was thinking, she ran a finger across her lip and then folded her hands on the table in front of her. "Were you hoping I'd come back?"

He hadn't expected such a bold question. He wasn't quite ready to answer it either. "Did you ever consider it?"

They stared at each other for several heartbeats, each willing the other to answer their question, before she broke eye contact and shrugged. "I wouldn't have had time to play even if I'd taken it with me." There was a hint of sadness in her voice. Maybe even regret.

Yep, he knew those feelings well himself. "You've always been a talented pianist. It bothers me that you don't play anymore. What happened to your dream of teaching piano lessons? Or sharing that love with others?"

Peyton laughed, but there was little humor in the sound. "Real life happened. You know, a divorce. A sister who was in all kinds of trouble. I was starting to find my footing in Houston when Trina found out she was pregnant. She had a lot of health issues during the pregnancy, so I quit my nine-to-five and got a job where the hours were more flexible. I could work while she was sleeping and help her during the day."

"At a grocery store."

She shrugged as though it were no big deal, but he caught the moisture in her eyes right before she looked away from him.

Before their divorce, she'd been a manager at a local restaurant and played the piano. There was nothing wrong with working at a grocery store. But for Peyton to go to working nights at one... It irked him. Did Trina not care that her sister had given everything up to help her?

Guilt at his negative thoughts toward the murdered woman helped rein in his frustration.

There was nothing he could do to retroactively make things better. A fact he'd come to accept with regard to their marriage, too.

Peyton took a bite of her doughnut and chewed thoughtfully. When she swallowed, her attention swiveled back to him. "I'm really glad you're practicing medicine. Seems like you've got a good place at the clinic. I was afraid that, after Afghanistan, after your injury, you might not want to anymore."

"I didn't. Not at first." Not for a while. "But the counseling helped. It made me see that there was so much good I could accomplish. So I chose to focus on that." It was the truth, but that made it sound so easy. It had been anything but. "It's been good."

"I'm happy for you, Jay. Truly." She spoke the truth but there was a sadness in her eyes.

"What you've done for Trina. For Rosie. It's more than admirable. Being there for family isn't easy." No doubt he and his brother would've been at each other's throats if they'd been forced to spend so much time together. He reached across the table and covered her hand with his. "But you've got a true talent in music. I hope it's something you can focus on again. You deserve it."

She looked at their hands and slowly lifted her chin until her gaze tangled with his. For half a moment, she started to nibble her lower lip, then realized what she was doing. "Maybe the time for that has passed. I've got Rosie now. Music is too unpredictable. I need to be able to support her. Support us." Her voice faltered, and she swallowed, shaking her head. "I need to be practical. Music isn't going to pay the bills."

He brushed his thumb across hers, and the connection strengthened the tension between them. "Just promise me you won't give up on it."

She slipped her hand out from beneath his. "Sometimes things don't work out the way we'd planned. Sometimes they can't be fixed." She got to her feet.

Jay stood. "Peyton. That's not what I'm trying to do."

She seemed to look everywhere but at him until she finally met his eyes again. "I know. Look, I'm going to check on Rosie. I'm surprised she's still asleep." With that, she retreated and disappeared down the hallway.

Jay released a lungful of air. He wanted to kick himself. Having Peyton here in his house was messing with him. He had no right to ask her to promise him anything, even if he did want to see her get back to music. It hurt knowing she'd given it up after the divorce. Sure, it was her choice. She could've started playing piano again at any time, but he couldn't help but feel at least partially responsible for it.

"I don't even know if it's possible to sort through this mess, God, but I miss having Peyton in my life. Even if we walk away as friends, it would be a huge answer to prayer."

He'd just stood and started to pack up the donuts when Peyton's scream pierced the air.

Moments later, he ran into the guest room and found her standing, facing the window, with one hand covering her mouth.

"Peyton? What happened?"

She waved toward the window, sunlight pouring in through the panes. "Someone was standing outside the window."

Chapter Fifteen

T he sound of Rosie's distressed cries drew Peyton to the crib. No doubt her own scream had scared the baby. She scooped Rosie into her arms and followed Jay to his bedroom. He withdrew a handgun from the safe by his bed and walked back out.

Peyton snagged his arm. "What if he's still out there?"

"I hope he is." He turned to look at her just long enough to say, "Stay inside with Rosie. I'll be right back."

She followed him as far as the living room but stopped as the front door closed behind him. She held Rosie close and rocked her back and forth while praying silently for Jay's safety. What if whoever was staring in the window was waiting for Jay outside? What if it was someone from Houston?

Peyton barely breathed until the door opened again, and Jay came inside. She noticed he'd tucked the gun into his waistband as he locked the door again.

"It's okay," he assured her. "It was the teen boy next door. He and a friend were playing basketball. The ball rolled in front of the house. I think you probably scared him about as badly as he scared you. He apologized. Repeatedly."

She closed her eyes as relief flooded her system. The poor kid—she could imagine how frightened he must've been, too. Rosie fussed in her arms. "What if it had been one of the men who killed Trina? What if they'd followed me here, and I put you at risk?" She looked at him then. Just thinking about the possibilities tied her stomach in knots. "I should have thought things through better before I pulled you into the middle of this. I should have..."

His eyes widened, his brows lifting. "You should have what?"

The truth was, she wasn't sure what else she could have done.

The realization must have shown on her face because Jay strode across the room until he was standing toe-to-toe with her. "Coming here was the right thing. We're going to get this figured out." He reached up and softly tucked several strands of her hair behind one ear, his hand lingering on her cheek for a moment before it dropped again.

Rosie let out a dissatisfied squeal before starting to suck on her own fingers.

Peyton went to work making a bottle, then watched as Rosie immediately latched onto the nipple. Her nose was still a little stuffy, but nothing like it had been. The fever was gone, too. Thank goodness.

Peyton pressed a kiss to her niece's forehead and settled into the recliner to feed her.

A few minutes later, Jay sat on the couch nearby, his phone to his ear. "Hold on, Logan. Let me put you on speaker." He did just that and held the phone out. "We're both here. Go ahead."

Logan's voice filled the living room. "Hey, Peyton. I was

able to gain access to your sister's phone. First of all, I wanted you to know that I saved all of the photos and videos for you. I'll get an SD card to you as soon as I can."

Tears sprang to her eyes. She hadn't realized just how worried she'd been that she might lose them until Logan told her that. "Thank you so much."

"Of course. There were surprisingly few people in her contacts. You, of course. Jeb and Stephen were both in there, too. There was also a Cindy Taylor. Do you know who that is?"

"Yes, that's Trina's boss."

He listed several other men by name, none of whom sounded familiar to Peyton. She told Logan as much as she lifted Rosie to her shoulder and patted her back. "Were there any texts that she may have gotten before she texted me that night?" She forcibly blocked the chain of events from her mind. Her gaze drifted to the piano, and she imagined running her fingers over the keys.

"Not that night. But there was one earlier in the day from an unknown number that was significant. It said, 'You're out of time.' There were no other texts from unknown numbers that were saved on the phone."

Jay exchanged a glance with Peyton. "So either Trina deleted the texts, or most of her interaction with that individual was done in person."

"I'm inclined to go with the latter." There was some shuffling in the background of the phone call. "I'd like to get a list of all phone calls and texts that came in and out of the phone, but I'd need a warrant. Right now, since we're keeping everything on the down-low, that's something I won't be able to get."

Peyton leaned toward Jay and the phone he still held. "I understand. Thank you, Logan."

"Not a problem. There's one more thing. I was able to locate Jeb Carter. He's living in New Hampshire now, and it looks like that's been the case for the last six months. We can look into alibis if it comes to that, but for right now, I don't think he's at the top of our suspect list. I'm sorry I didn't find more. Let me know if there's anything else I can do."

"Thanks again, man." Jay ended the call and set the phone on the coffee table.

Peyton set the empty bottle on the side table and laid Rosie on her lap. The baby gave her a big, gummy smile. A little milk dripped from one corner of her mouth. Peyton smiled back and tickled her niece's chin. Rosie's pretty brown eyes were so much like Trina's.

Jay cleared his throat. For a minute there, Peyton had nearly forgotten he was sitting on the couch.

"I got a text from Bryce a few minutes ago. He and Megan offered to bring an early dinner and stay for a bit. I don't want you to feel pressured, but I know all the waiting has been hard today. Maybe it'd be a good way to pass the time while we wait to hear back from Nate's contact. I may see if Nate would like to drop by, too." He held up a hand. "But only if it's something you feel up for."

He was right. The waiting was horrible. The morning had stretched on, and it was barely ten o'clock. It was also Saturday. What were the odds that Nate's contact would reach out to him over the weekend?

"I think that sounds great."

"Are you sure?"

When she nodded, a smile brightened his face. "I'll let Bryce know."

95

Peyton looked around the living room full of people. Bryce and Megan had shown up with dinner at four o'clock. They brought fish and chips, something Megan said the baby had been craving for the last two months solid. Bryce had placed a loving hand on his wife's abdomen, laughed, and joked that they should've invested in the restaurant for as often as he's going by and picking up food for his wife.

Peyton had no complaints. The food was delicious.

She'd had her doubts about trying to focus enough to visit with the couple, but having them there was a wonderful distraction. It was entertaining to watch the way Jay and Bryce joked back and forth. Then, there was the loving way that Bryce and Megan kept interacting with each other. They'd all included Peyton as though she'd never left Destiny two years ago.

The men were laughing about something. Megan looked over at Peyton and shook her head in mock worry. "I have a feeling this little guy is going to be just like his daddy. Heaven help me." She gave her husband a loving look.

Peyton smiled. There was no doubt the baby would be so very loved. "Do you have a name picked out yet?"

"Not yet. We have a few ideas, but we've decided to wait and choose something after we see him."

Not long after they'd finished eating, Nate returned to the house with Minnie. Logan pulled in at the same time.

When Peyton had pictured the technology expert in her mind, she imagined a tall, thin guy who was shy. Logan was about as opposite that as he could have been. The man might have been a bodybuilder. He approached Peyton and held out an SD card.

"I wanted to make sure you got those photos and videos right away." He gave her a gentle smile.

"Thank you." She accepted the card.

One day, she had every intention of looking at the contents, but it might be a while before she was ready. She left to put it somewhere safe in the guest room.

When she returned, she chose a spot on the floor next to Minnie the Rottweiler, who was lying on her back. The dog welcomed the belly rubs, her tongue lolling from one side of her mouth.

What was it about petting the animal that made Peyton feel more relaxed? She'd already decided that, once life stabilized and she had a good house for herself and Rosie, she would get a dog. Peyton had never had a pet, but she wanted Rosie to grow up with one. Maybe she'd look for a dog like Minnie. It wouldn't hurt to have a protector like her guarding the house.

Minnie jumped to her feet and started licking Peyton's cheek as though the dog could read her mind and was giving her full support.

Nate snapped his fingers, and Minnie sat down, casting her owner a wounded look.

"I don't mind," Peyton assured him. "She's not bothering me."

Jay was chuckling. "You'd better be careful, Nate. I think Minnie just might have chosen a new favorite human."

Everyone else laughed.

As though Minnie understood every word and wanted to reassure her owner, she trotted over and licked Nate's hand.

Megan had been holding Rosie when the baby fell asleep. She ran a hand over the little one's head. "I don't know how she manages to sleep with all of this noise."

Bryce reached over and gave her arm an affectionate squeeze. "Are you kidding? I think you're the queen of sleeping through anything."

She laughed with a shake of her head. "That's thanks to being seven months pregnant and working twelve-hour shifts at the hospital." She looked at Peyton. "Trust me, it is not the norm."

Jay stood. "Here, why don't I go put Rosie down in the other room?"

Megan looked like she wanted to object, but she also seemed like she needed to shift positions. She relinquished the baby with a look of longing.

Peyton watched Jay as he gently lifted Rosie and carried her into the other room.

When he returned, he insisted that Peyton take his spot on the couch before moving to sit on the hearth.

The group of friends swapped stories and inside jokes, and while Peyton didn't have much to contribute, she was content to listen and laugh. It'd been a long time since she felt comfortable like this. Most of her interactions with Trina had been like walking a thin line between ignoring behavior that she knew would harm her sister and pointing it out, which often earned her Trina's anger. Things got a little better once Rosie was born, but that was mostly because there was someone else for them to focus their attention on.

Guilt turned sour in her stomach. Not just for allowing herself to enjoy this time with new friends, but because of the negative thoughts that had entered her mind. It didn't matter how different they were, Peyton would give anything for Trina to still be alive. Even more, she would have loved for her to be surrounded by people like this—friends who cared about and were there for each other.

She glanced at Jay as he laughed, his eyes sparkling.

It was nice to see him this way, too. When he'd come back from his last tour in Afghanistan, he'd been injured, but the emotional toll was more noticeable than the physical. He'd been withdrawn. Sullen. It'd broken her heart, but there didn't seem to be any way to truly reach him then. She was thankful he'd found a way to heal. She just wished she could've been a part of the process.

If she and Trina had grown up with a group of friends or family like this, how would their lives have turned out differently? Trina might have been happier. Healthier.

She might still be alive.

But Peyton might never have met Jay. As hard as their divorce was, she wouldn't trade the good moments of their marriage for anything. Rosie might not be here, either.

The possibilities were endless, and there were trade-offs no matter how she looked at it.

Her head ached, and she forcibly pushed the thoughts aside.

What was done was done. There was no going back. No changing the past.

She caught Jay watching her with concern. Thankfully, he said nothing, and no one else seemed to pick up on her melancholy mood. She tried to focus on what the others were saying and laugh appropriately.

Her phone rang with an incoming call, startling her. She pulled it from her back pocket and silenced it. "Unknown" flashed on the screen. Most likely a spam call. She rejected it and set the phone on the floor by her knee.

A moment later, it started to ring again. The same "Unknown" popped up on the screen. She rejected the call again, but this time, an uneasy knot formed in the pit of her stomach.

Her phone pinged with a text. It was from the same unknown number.

She was tempted to ignore it, too, but instinct told her to click on it.

Answer your phone.

Chapter Sixteen

For a while, Peyton had seemed to relax and even enjoy herself as everyone joked and laughed. But at some point, her smiles had become forced. Sad.

Jay had been on the verge of bringing the gathering to an end when she got a phone call. She didn't answer it.

A few moments later, she looked at the screen, and her face blanched.

"Peyton?"

Everyone else had stopped talking and was trying to figure out what was going on.

Jay stood and walked toward her. As he approached, she held the phone out to him, her hand shaking.

He read the text on the screen.

Answer your phone.

"I didn't recognize the number, so I blocked the call." Peyton looked nervous.

The phone began to ring again. Jay lifted it. "Answer, and put it on speaker." He handed it back to her.

She nodded and swallowed hard, then swiped to answer. She put it on speaker. "Hello?"

"Is this Peyton Kennedy?"

She tensed. "What do you want?"

"I want the money. And you're going to give it to me."

"I don't even know what you're talking about. What money?"

Jay placed a steadying hand on her shoulder and gave it a gentle squeeze.

"Your sister stole a great deal of money, and you're going to bring it to me."

Peyton shook her head. "I told you, I don't have any money. If Trina did take it, she never told me about it."

The man on the other end of the call increased the volume of his voice. "You have forty-eight hours. If that money isn't in my hands, I will drive to Destiny myself, find your ex-husband and that little brat, and I will kill them both. Do you understand?"

Peyton's mouth opened, but no words came out. She passed a panicked look to Jay. He reached for her hand and gave her a nod. "Yes... yes. I understand."

"Don't even think about giving the money over to the police. If you screw this up, you will regret it. Forty-eight hours. I'll contact you with a drop-off location."

With that, the call ended.

Peyton let go of Jay's hand and crossed her arms in front of her. "His voice. It was one of the guys at Trina's house."

Someone was threatening Peyton and Rosie, and they had no idea who it was.

Jay took the phone from her and handed it to Nate.

"At least now we know what they're looking for." Nate passed the phone to Logan, who grabbed it and his laptop and went to the kitchen table without a word.

Peyton stood, but the moment Jay moved toward her,

she put up a hand to stop him. "I'm going to go check on Rosie. I just need a few minutes." She tried to muster a smile but failed miserably.

Jay let her go with every intention to check on her in a few minutes if she didn't return.

Nate went to join Logan at the table, leaving Megan and Bryce waiting for an explanation. Jay hadn't wanted to bring them into the situation because the fewer people who knew, the better, but it was too late now. And he knew Bryce well enough to know that his friend would insist on helping.

As briefly as possible, he told them what had happened to Peyton in Houston and what the situation looked like now.

"As disturbing as this call was, at least now we have some answers." Jay glanced at the hallway and wondered how long he should wait before checking on Peyton.

Nate spoke up from the kitchen table. "Logan is trying to trace the number."

Bryce went to stand beside the recliner and reached for Megan's hand. "I can't even imagine." He leaned down and pressed a kiss to his wife's head. "What can we do?"

"Honestly? I'm not sure there's anything you can do. I was hoping she could fly under the radar while we waited for the investigations to continue in Houston. But now..."

Peyton re-entered the living room, paced to the fire-place, then turned around. "I'm going back."

The room fell silent. Even the faint clacking of the keyboard in the kitchen stopped.

Jay shook his head. "Absolutely not. There's no way you're going back to Houston—they'll be waiting for you."

"And if I don't, they'll come here instead." She spread

her arms. "Since they know I'm in Destiny, it wouldn't take much to connect me to you. It's not safe to be here anymore."

Jay hated that she was right. He turned to look at Nate and Logan. "Any luck tracing the number?"

Logan frowned. "Unfortunately not. It was a pre-paid burner phone, so tracking the buyer will be next to impossible. The guy probably uses the phone for this type of communication. This isn't his first rodeo." He tilted his head slightly. "With the right setup, we can try to track him next time the phone is turned on, but it'll have to be active longer than it takes to send a text for me to do that."

"It's certainly worth a try." Nate ran a hand through his thick hair. "Patterson has had next to no luck getting any information in Houston so far. He hasn't given up, though." He gave Jay a look that said he wished he could do more.

"I don't think I have much of a choice, then." Peyton crossed her arms in front of her and lifted her chin.

"It's too risky." Jay wasn't going to back down.

Her eyes flashed, and she widened her stance. "There's nothing we can do about it from here. This isn't something you can just fix, Jay. If I don't go back, the only alternative is to take Rosie, disappear, and hope they never track us down."

"Running away isn't the solution, either." Why couldn't she see that? Anger flared. "Do you really want to be looking over your shoulder for the rest of your life?"

She didn't even blink at his raised voice.

"At least I'd be alive. Rosie, too. It's certainly better than just sitting here waiting for them to strike."

Bryce had pulled his phone out and was showing something to Megan. They were clearly trying to look busy and pretend they weren't listening to the conversation. The same went for Nate and Logan, who were both focusing way too much on the laptop screen.

Jay motioned to the hallway. "Can we talk in the other room, please?"

She hesitated a moment, then nodded.

He led the way into his office, waited until she came inside, and closed the door behind her to give them a little more privacy and spare his friends the drama.

She was glaring at him, her arms pressed tightly against her sides. Her green eyes flashed, and she seemed braced for what he was about to say next.

He took several breaths and prayed that he could find the right words to express what he was thinking instead of reacting with knee-jerk responses. "I apologize if I'm coming off like I'm trying to fix your situation. Or like I'm trying to control you. That's not my intention. I'm truly worried for your safety—and Rosie's—if you go back to Houston. They want that money, and unless you've been holding out on me, you don't have it. You need a plan in place. Not only to keep yourselves safe but to figure out who's behind all of this."

Peyton's shoulders relaxed a little, and so did her stance. "I really have no intention of running away, either. I want to figure out who killed Trina and make them pay. Rosie deserves to grow up in a stable environment."

Her eyes filled with tears, and she blinked rapidly. "But you're right. It's not safe to take Rosie back with me. I was hoping..." She stalled and shifted her feet. "I was hoping I could leave her here with you until all of this is finished. I know she'd be safe with you and that you'd take good care of her."

Jay's eyes widened. He hadn't seen that coming. The fact that she was willing to trust him with Rosie's care, even in the face of the possibility that Peyton might not make it back, was not lost on him.

He shoved his hands into the pockets of his jeans to keep himself from reaching for her. "I would. I'd protect her with my life. But I know, with every fiber of my being, that I can't let you go back to Houston alone." Images flashed in his mind as his imagination ran with deadly possibilities. "If I stayed here, and something happened to you, I would never be able to forgive myself."

She shook her head and pressed her lips together. "And if you came with me, and something happened to you…" With a groan, she jabbed the fingers of both hands into her hair at the scalp and tipped her head back.

Her arms dropped to her sides again. They spent several seconds staring at each other. Jay focused on the rise and fall of her shoulders as she breathed deeply. Determination flashed in her eyes with a slight shadow of fear.

At that moment, he wanted nothing more than to step forward, pull her into his arms, and kiss her until they both forgot the danger. He knew what holding her felt like. Knew how addicting it was.

Knew that he didn't have the right to hold her anymore. Regret slammed into his chest, and he resisted the urge to rub the spot above his heart.

"I'm coming with you, Peyton." He had no intention of backing down. If she insisted on going back alone, he would follow her anyway.

She must have seen the truth because she finally gave a small nod of agreement.

Some of the tension drained from his shoulders. "But we can't take Rosie with us. We'll talk to Bryce and Megan and see if they can keep her. If not, maybe Erica."

"Okay." Her voice was barely above a whisper. She crossed her arms in front of her as though she were cold.

"Okay." He led the way out of the office and back to the living room.

Nate was sitting perched on the arm of the couch, clearly waiting for them to return. "All right, so what's the plan?"

Chapter Seventeen

Peyton stood at the window, the curtain pulled back and watched until Bryce and Megan's car drove out of sight. She pictured Rosie tucked into her car seat in the back of their vehicle, and her arms felt suddenly empty. Tears threatened to fall as she prayed that she'd see her niece again soon.

"They'll keep her safe." Jay's voice came from behind her.

"I know." She sniffed.

She had no doubt that the couple would care for Rosie. Plus, they'd reassured her that if they ran into any trouble at all, they had backup. It turned out that two of Bryce's friends worked for the Abilene Police Department, and one of them was the chief.

Did she doubt that Rosie would be safe? No. But she *did* hate having to hand the baby over like this. Especially so soon after Trina... Rosie was too young to understand what was going on, but Peyton still worried she'd feel abandoned.

She took a steadying breath and turned to find Jay standing there, waiting for her. There was no pity in his eyes. No judgment. Instead, there was unmistakable respect and understanding.

Before she could second-guess herself, Peyton strode toward him. He opened his arms and pulled her close. She rested her cheek against his chest as he wrapped his arms around her.

"Father God," he began, his voice steady, "we come before You and ask that You surround Rosie with Your love and protection. Guide us as we navigate through these uncertain waters and keep us safe as well. Help us somehow find justice for Trina. Bring Peyton and Rosie back together again. In the name of Jesus, Your precious Son's name, we pray. Amen."

"Amen," Peyton whispered.

"Amen." Nate spoke from his spot at the kitchen table.

Peyton took in a deep, steadying breath and then stepped out of Jay's arms. She found Nate watching them. Warmth flooded her cheeks, and she refused to look at Jay, who pressed a soft kiss to her hair.

It was just the three of them now. Logan had left with a promise to be available if they got any more information they needed him to run.

Nate volunteered to go with them to Houston. After all, he knew Lee Patterson and thought the connection plus close approximation might help when it came to getting information from the police department. In the meantime, they'd have someone else there to watch their backs.

He wasn't wrong. They decided to take his vehicle. Once in Houston, they'd rent another for Peyton and Jay to use, and Nate would put their motel rooms in his name.

Peyton insisted on paying him back once she could. Nate had only given her a shake of his head and said, "Don't worry, I'll hold this guy over here responsible." Then he'd given Jay a friendly shove.

It didn't matter who ended up footing the bill. Peyton would make sure they got every penny back as soon as she was able.

It would take them less than four hours to drive to Houston from Destiny. They planned to leave early tomorrow so they could get there by eight in the morning. Peyton knew she needed to sleep tonight, but between Rosie being gone and not knowing what was going to happen tomorrow, she suspected it wouldn't be easy.

Nate leaned his dining room chair back until it was balanced on two legs. "We need to talk about the money. Do you think Trina might have had it like they're saying she did?"

He gave Peyton an apologetic look. Minnie got up from her spot in the living room and went to sit beside him, welcoming the ear scratches that he dished out.

"I've been thinking about that ever since the phone call." She shrugged. "Truthfully, I think it could go either way. She was struggling financially. She liked to be taken care of by the man of the month. I'm finding it difficult to reconcile the idea of her straight up stealing a huge sum of money, but if someone gave it to her..." Peyton frowned. "I think it's possible. This seems like a lot of effort to go through if they weren't certain."

Jay walked into the kitchen and opened a cabinet. "I tend to agree. Whether she was aware of it or not, I think she had the money in her possession at some point." He held up a container of chocolate chip cookies.

"That's what I'm talking about." Nate righted his chair. "You got some milk?"

"Yep." Jay grabbed three glasses and a carton of milk

from the fridge, and brought all of it to the table. "Help yourselves."

Peyton had never been big on dipping cookies in milk. But the cookies themselves? Yes, please. "Thank you." She bit into one and let the sugary chocolate goodness melt on her tongue. What was it about chocolate that seemed to make almost anything more tolerable?

Trina used to laugh and tease her about being a choco-holic. Peyton supposed she was, but there were worse things to be addicted to. Right?

Nate filled his glass with milk, dunked the cookie up to his finger and thumb, and ate it in one bite. When he swallowed, he asked, "Let's go on the assumption that Trina did have the money. Can you think of anywhere she might have hidden it? Any place in the house where she stored valuables?"

With a slow shake of her head, Peyton tried to search her memory for anything that sounded likely. Trina had been reluctant to share personal things with Peyton. Unless, of course, it was about how great her latest boyfriend was. Ugh, she hated these negative thoughts about her sister. The guilt stung, and tears pricked at her eyes.

"She never told me about anything. I know she was struggling financially. We both were." She made a point of not looking directly at Jay. She didn't want to see anything remotely related to pity. "I suggested I move into her house, and we could share the rent. She refused and said she needed space."

It'd hurt Peyton's feelings at the time. Sometimes, it felt like she practically lived there anyway. Although, in hindsight, it'd probably been for the best.

Neither Jay nor Nate said anything. She appreciated the time to think as she finished her first cookie.

"I feel like, if she used something typical like a safe or a jewelry box, they would have found it already. You know?"

Jay nodded. "It makes sense. If we can get back into the house, do you feel comfortable looking around? Seeing if there's anything that stands out as unusual? It might be something as silly as a cookie jar that never had cookies in it or a mason jar on the top shelf of a cabinet."

Could she handle going into the house again? An image of Trina on the living room floor flashed in her mind, and Peyton flinched. She wasn't sure. Except that, if finding her sister's killers hinged on it, she'd find a way to push through.

"I'll do my best."

They sat in silence for several moments as everyone munched thoughtfully on their cookies.

Peyton did a mental run-through of Trina's house. She tried to picture every shelf. Every cabinet. She attempted to remember the contents of every closet she'd been in right down to Rosie's.

Wait.

She paused, her cookie halfway to her mouth, as she thought back over her frenzied escape from the house. She'd grabbed that open canister of formula from the shelf on the changing table.

Trina normally stored the formula in the kitchen...

Peyton set her cookie on the table and jumped to her feet. "I'll be right back."

Chapter Eighteen

Peyton abandoned her cookie and hurried from the room. Jay was just about to go and check on her when she returned, and there was a canister of formula in her hands. Both he and Nate leaned forward.

She set it on the table with a thud. "I grabbed this from Rosie's room when I was trying to get out of the house after..." Her voice caught. She swallowed and continued. "I remember being thankful because the formula is normally in the kitchen. If this hadn't been there, I wouldn't have had anything with me to make Rosie a bottle."

Peyton strode to the counter and reached for the roll of paper towels. She laid a line of them out on the kitchen table.

"The weird thing was that the canister had already been opened, but it didn't look like Trina had used any of it. At the time, I just thought it was a small miracle. Now, I'm wondering..."

"...if she hid something in it." Jay finished the thought and stood. "That's not a bad idea."

"Or I'm desperate."

Jay didn't think so. Maybe this was nothing, but it was worth checking out. He retrieved a colander and a large measuring cup. "Here, we can pour it back in if there's nothing but formula. That way, we don't waste it."

She nodded her thanks, set the colander on top of the measuring cup, and began to pour the formula.

Jay wasn't sure what he expected, but he'd half-hoped for a roll of money or something. Instead, he was just about to think there was nothing unusual in it when something gold fell out with the last of the powder.

A shake of the colander revealed a key that clattered in the bottom.

Peyton dumped it out onto the paper towel.

"May I?" Jay nodded at the key.

She shifted the paper towel toward him.

He picked it up and studied both sides. "It might go to a lockbox. Maybe a safe deposit box at a bank." He handed it to Nate.

"Maybe. There's no bank name on it, but then again, maybe there wouldn't be." Nate took a picture of both sides of the key. The number 202 was etched into it. "I'll send these pictures to Logan. See if he can figure out where the key came from."

He handed the key back to Peyton. She lifted it up and down in her hand as though studying its weight, but her gaze was fixed on something in the distance.

Jay resisted the urge to reach out and touch her. "What are you thinking?"

She looked up in surprise. There was a hint of hope in her eyes that quickly gave way to grief. "I guess I was thinking that if this really does lead to the money, then maybe the men who killed Trina will be behind bars soon. Then I'll be putting one nightmare behind me so I can face another one." Her shoulders fell. "There's so much to consider with Rosie. So many decisions. How do I know what to do?"

"You take it one step at a time. Sometimes, those steps aren't on level ground. Sometimes, they're across jagged rocks or footholds going up a cliff wall. It doesn't matter what the terrain is as long as you're moving forward. You'll gain clarity along the way, and eventually get to where you need to be."

Peyton blinked at him. "That was surprisingly insightful."

He shrugged. "I have my moments."

Nate chuckled. "Though they are few and far between."

"Funny." Jay shot him a look of mock annoyance. The truth was, he and Nate had traveled some of that rough ground together at times. Making the trek with a friend or loved one always helped.

He thought back to his rocky marriage with Peyton. That had been a big part of their problem—they'd tried to make the journey alone. Or at least argued about which path to take. No wonder they eventually wandered too far from each other to find their way back. There were a lot of things he knew now that he wished he'd known back then.

They finished their cookies. Nate took Minnie and headed to drop her off with a friend, get a few hours of sleep, and meet them back at the house early in the morning.

Jay made sure the house was locked down and went to take a quick shower. Peyton said she was going to try to rest. But when he turned the water off, the sound of the piano floated through the air.

He listened to the music as he toweled off and changed

into lounge pants and a T-shirt. He'd missed this so much. Peyton used to play all the time, and the sound of the piano had been a staple in their home. After their divorce, there'd been times he could've sworn he'd heard it even when he knew it was impossible.

Afraid she might stop playing, he silently re-entered the living room and leaned against the wall in the doorway.

She sat on the bench, her delicate fingers dancing over the keys as she played a beautiful rendition of Amazing Grace. Her eyes were closed. Tears slid unhindered down her cheeks.

He felt a prickle behind his own eyes. Silently, he prayed for this woman and all the grief that was overwhelming her. Prayed that God would reach down and ease some of her burdens.

The song ended, and when Peyton opened her eyes again, she swiped at her tears. Her gaze swung to him. "Hey."

"Hey." He walked across the room and sat on the end of the couch closest to the piano. "That was beautiful."

"Thank you." She lifted her hands. "I guess it's like riding a bike."

He wasn't surprised. Playing the piano had been like breathing for her. No matter what happened in the next few days, he'd make sure she got that piano if he had to rent a trailer and take it to Houston himself.

It would help her as she went through the grieving process, and Rosie should grow up in a home full of music.

Jay's heart ached, but he refused to analyze why. He glanced at the clock. It was after eleven. "You should try to get some sleep." Nate would be back at four, and hopefully, they'd be able to get going shortly afterward.

"Yeah." She looked at the piano longingly, touched the

keys, and then lowered the cover. She pushed the bench back and stood. She headed for the guest room, and he followed.

Peyton paused in the doorway. "I hope Rosie is doing okay for Bryce and Megan."

"She's probably fast asleep right now."

She nodded but didn't step into the room. "It feels so empty." She leaned her head against the doorframe.

"We're going to get this figured out. Rosie will be back with you soon." Of that, Jay was certain. He and Nate weren't going to allow any other outcome if they could help it. But he just wished he knew what that meant for Peyton. If she would be living in Houston or hiding out somewhere else.

He leaned forward and placed a kiss on her cheek. "Get some rest, Peyton."

She nodded and yawned. "You, too."

Jay left her then and went to his own room. The moment he lay down, his brain started running through various possibilities for tomorrow. It was some time before he finally fell asleep.

Chapter Nineteen

They were on the road before five the next morning. Nate drove his silver Dodge Ram. Even though Jay had offered for Peyton to take shotgun, she insisted he do so. She was riding in the back seat that was nearly packed with luggage, a cooler of food, and other supplies that he and Nate had put together.

The drive had been completely uneventful. Even still, Jay kept an eye on the rearview mirror and any vehicles at the rest areas where they stopped. He could tell Nate was doing the same.

"You doing okay back there?" Nate asked as he rose up to look in the rearview mirror at Peyton.

"I'm good. Better. I feel like at least we're being proactive."

Jay understood completely. There was nothing worse than being in a situation and just waiting for something to happen.

Nate nodded. "I called and reserved a couple of hotel rooms on the same side of town as your apartment." And Trina's house, though he hadn't said that. "I have one with two queens and another with a single bed. I was hoping to get them connected, but it turns out that isn't a super common thing anymore. Who knew?"

"That'll work. We can get checked in, pick up the rental car, and go from there."

They were still waiting to hear from Logan about the key. He hadn't been able to find much online. He was hoping to do some more investigating from Destiny, but since it was Sunday, he likely wouldn't have answers until Monday. If the key *did* belong to a safe deposit box, banks would be closed today, too.

Once they got set up, Nate was going to reach out to Detective Parker and see if they could arrange a meeting. Maybe then he could get more definitive answers.

Most likely, Jay and Peyton would be waiting at the hotel for a while. Eventually, though, going through Trina's house was likely their main goal for the day. It was necessary, but the idea of going back to the scene of the crime made Jay nervous. They'd be fools if they thought the place wasn't being watched by the people who were after Peyton as well as the police. Getting inside without being seen would be tricky.

But one thing at a time.

They pulled into the hotel parking lot. Nate went inside to get them checked in and then drove around to the back of the building and parked in front of their hotel rooms. "Okay, we've got rooms 173 and 174. The double is 174." He reached for the key cards that would unlock the doors and handed one to Peyton.

Jay and Nate had talked about the rooms. Of course, Peyton should have the single. That said, he would feel much better if the rooms had been adjoining.

Peyton unlocked her door and moved to the side so Jay

could carry her bag in. When he'd turned around again, she hadn't moved.

"What is it?" He looked around the room. It seemed clean. And for a run-of-the-mill hotel room, it was relatively nice. There was even a small refrigerator and a microwave.

"I know this is silly, but is there any chance that you and I could share the other hotel room? Separate beds, of course." She rushed through that second sentence, and her cheeks turned pink. "It'd make me feel better."

"Are you kidding? It'd make me feel better, too. I'd prefer to be nearby, but I didn't want to make you uncomfortable. Give me a minute to talk to Nate."

The look of relief on her face mirrored how he felt.

Nate not only had zero objections, but he preferred the arrangement as well. They got luggage distributed between the two rooms. He handed his truck keys over to Jay. "Just in case you need it. I'll take the hotel shuttle over to the car rental company and be back as soon as I can. Holler if something comes up."

"Will do." Jay shut and locked the door behind his friend, then pocketed the keys. When he turned, his injured leg protested.

Peyton frowned. "Is it bothering you after the drive?"

"A little. It'll work itself out now that I'm moving around." He hated that she'd even noticed the limp in the first place. The last thing he'd ever wanted was to look weak in front of her, which was why he refused help when he first got home from Afghanistan and why he avoided the topic entirely.

She looked like she wanted to say something else but pressed her lips together instead. Her gaze flicked to his leg, his eyes, and then across the room to the door.

He would've been happy to let the moment go, except

that's exactly what he'd done with her before. Instead, he gave her what he hoped was an encouraging smile. "What else were you wondering about?"

Peyton's eyebrows rose in shock, although she covered it quickly. "Do you still go to physical therapy for it?"

When they'd divorced, he'd been in the midst of therapy sessions to try and help bring full strength to the muscles in his leg.

"Not anymore. I haven't for about a year now. I do have some exercises I have to do regularly to keep things loose. Sitting in the car for over four hours made it tight. Walking around like this will make it feel better soon." He was thankful he didn't need a cane or anything to assist him. Back when he'd first gotten back to the States, it had been a worry.

"I'm really glad to hear that." The expression on her face was sincere as she took a seat on one of the beds. "I know it bothered you when I asked about what happened overseas. After a while, I quit asking. But I wanted you to know that the reason I asked was because I cared. Because I didn't know how to help you get to where you were going if I didn't know where you were coming from." The corners of her mouth dipped, and she picked at a spot on her right thumb. "I'm sorry I pushed so much in the beginning. I've wondered a thousand times if it would have made a difference if I had backed off. You know?"

"There's plenty of blame to go around. The truth of the matter is that we had communication problems. A lot of them. It was more than you asking me what happened or me refusing to talk." It'd taken a while—and a lot of blaming Peyton in addition to blaming himself—to realize that.

"I get what you mean. It was a combination of a lot of things. After a while, I think we got used to not asking. Not

121

opening up. Not caring." She sighed. "I wish I could go back in time and smack some sense into my younger self."

"So do I." He realized how that sounded and chuckled. "I mean, smack some sense into *my* younger self. Not yours."

She laughed with him. "Good to know."

Jay considered telling her what happened in Afghanistan, but the thought had no sooner entered his mind than his cell phone rang.

"It's Logan." He swiped the screen to answer and then put it on speaker. "Hey, I'm here with Peyton."

"Hey, guys. I just got pulled into a case, so I only have a minute. I'm still trying to investigate that key of yours. I haven't been able to figure out where it came from yet, but I can tell you that it doesn't appear to open a safe deposit box." Someone spoke in the background, and it sounded as though Logan had covered the phone for a moment. "As soon as this gets wrapped up, I'll look into lockers at gyms and the bus and subway stations. I've got to go. Don't hesitate to reach out if there's anything else you want me to check into. If I don't answer right off, I promise I still got the message. Be careful out there."

With that, the call ended before Jay had a chance to thank him.

"I was really hoping for a more definite answer." Peyton fell backward onto the bed, her arms wide, and released a heavy sigh. "If the key *does* belong to a locker somewhere, it'll be like looking for a needle in a haystack."

Chapter Twenty

They didn't have to wait long for Nate to return with the rental car, coffee, and breakfast sandwiches. Peyton munched on hers while she listened to the guys. Jay shared the phone call from Logan, and Nate informed them that he'd already heard back from Detective Patterson and was supposed to meet in person over an early lunch.

"I'm hoping, now that we're in the area, I can get more answers. Maybe he can even set up a meeting with Detective Abbott so I can ask some direct questions." Nate didn't look completely convinced, but he did sound more positive than he had earlier. He took a large bite of his sandwich.

"I wish we knew how long Logan will be tied up with the case he's working." Jay removed the lid from his cup and took a sip of coffee. Black, like always.

Peyton always had to add a lot of sugar to make her coffee palatable. Today, however, she probably would have downed it either way. She was in desperate need of a caffeine kick. "We can't just sit around here and wait. We need to do something. Look somewhere."

Jay ate the last bite of his sandwich and dusted his hands off on his pants with a nod. He grabbed his phone and a notepad and pen. "I was thinking about that." He gave Peyton a sympathetic look. "You and Trina lived and worked in a relatively small area of town. Sure, Trina could've hidden the money anywhere, but the odds are it was close by. So let's make a list of all gyms, bus stations, and any other place that might have a locker within a ten-mile radius. We can check those locations."

Having something to work on gave Peyton an energy boost that the coffee hadn't accomplished. "And if the key doesn't match any of those, we can go out another ten." She reached for the notepad and pen. "Here, you read out what you find, and I'll write them down."

Nate watched them in silence and ate his breakfast.

Twenty minutes later, Peyton looked at their list of six places with satisfaction. At the bottom, she added the restaurant where Trina had worked. "Just in case they had lockers for the employees to store their things in while they were working."

Nate had finished his food and downed the last of his coffee. "You need to avoid your apartment, Trina's house, and the restaurant. The people who are after the money will likely have someone watching all three."

Peyton had thought of that. "No doubt you're right. But if we can't make any headway, and Logan doesn't have much luck, we won't have a choice." She shivered at the thought of people watching them. She'd rather they didn't identify them and the rental car they were driving for as long as possible. "At the same time, going back to the restaurant or even the grocery store where I worked might mean I recognize the voice from the other night."

"I'm going to meet with Patterson. Keep your heads

down, and stick to the other businesses on your list. If we do need to kick the hornet's nest, we're going to do it together." Nate wadded up the paper from his sandwich and tossed it into the small wastebasket by the hotel door. "Three are better than two. Not just for watching each other's backs, but to deter someone from getting impatient before our forty-eight hours are up."

Jay gave his friend a nod. "I'm with you. We'll check these places out. Be as discrete as possible. Hopefully, either Detective Patterson or Logan will come up with more information in the meantime."

Peyton pointed. "There it is. Up ahead on the right."

The sign for Sal's Corner Gym was barely visible from the road, thanks to a line of trees that blocked the view. It was hard to tell whether the city was responsible for the trees or if they were private property, but they needed to be trimmed back regardless.

Jay pulled into the lot and put the little white Jetta in park.

Peyton could see people using ellipticals and stationary bikes through a series of long and tall windows. She couldn't even imagine Trina going to a gym. She might have chuckled at the idea if it weren't for the reality of the situation. The truth was, the only reason Trina would go into a gym would be to meet guys. Or, potentially, to hide a bunch of cash.

She looked down at her jeans and peasant-style blouse. "I'm not going to pass as someone dropping by to work out." She looked over at Jay. He, too, was wearing jeans along with a T-shirt that accentuated the muscles in his upper arms. Even if he wasn't dressed for the gym, at least he looked like he knew his way around one.

Her gaze lifted to find him watching her, an amused look on his face. Her cheeks immediately heated.

Jay chuckled. "That's because you look like someone who doesn't need to."

The compliment warmed her, and she suddenly felt like an awkward teenager around her favorite crush, which was absolutely ridiculous. Not only were they not together, but they were also divorced. She did not have a crush on him, although she'd be lying if she said she didn't still find him incredibly attractive. She felt her blush deepen and cleared her throat. "Let's go."

She was walking across the parking lot before Jay got out of the car. He jogged to catch up with her and hit the key fob to lock the car behind them.

"We'll go in as people interested in a membership and request a tour." Jay slowed his stride to match hers. "With any luck, we'll run into someone else in one of the locker rooms and be able to see what kind of key they're using."

"That sounds like a plan." She pulled the key out of her pocket and pressed it between her thumb and first finger. Hopefully, the 202 actually corresponded to a specific locker number instead of something random.

Jay opened the door and held it so Peyton could go in first. She'd half expected it to be warm and smell like sweat inside. Instead, cool air greeted them, along with a strong, spicy scent. Some kind of diffuser was running on the front counter, no doubt the source of the aroma.

He reached for Peyton's hand and held it in his as he addressed the guy manning the front desk. "Hi there. My wife and I are considering a gym membership. Would it be possible to take a look around? See what all your gym offers?"

The guy looked up from his phone. "We're a little short-handed today. I can give you a tour if you want to have a seat and wait for about ten minutes." He went back to his phone.

Peyton raised an eyebrow at Jay. The guy clearly wasn't doing anything else. She had to assume he wasn't supposed to leave the front desk unattended.

Jay gave her hand a squeeze. "Look, we only have a few minutes. Is there any chance we could just have a quick look around?"

The guy seemed annoyed to have to look up from his phone again. He took in their apparel, must have figured they weren't likely to start using the equipment, and gave a short nod. "Let me know if you have any questions."

"I appreciate it. Come on, honey, let's go see what kind of ellipticals they have." He tugged her hand and turned them away from the front desk.

They moved into the main area and strolled past different exercise equipment as though they were trying to evaluate the gym. There were cubicles to put bags or shoes in, but no lockers there.

Jay was still holding her hand, and Peyton couldn't quite make herself let his go. After everything she'd gone through over the last few days, that connection with Jay was calming. Reassuring. She wasn't quite ready to give it up.

They got to the other side where the restrooms and lockers were located.

Peyton tipped her head toward the sign that boldly stated WOMEN on it. "I'll go take a look."

He nodded his head. "I'll be right out here."

Only then did he release her hand. Cool air danced over

her palm, and she plunged it into her pocket to retrieve the key.

The locker room was brightly lit. The floral air freshener was nearly overwhelming, but she preferred it to the smell of sweaty socks.

One entire wall was filled with blue lockers. Peyton was thankful that another woman was there. It looked like she'd just finished her workout. Her hair was in disarray, and her face red as she tossed a towel onto a nearby bench.

Peyton pulled out her phone and pretended to look at it as the woman used a key to open her locker. The key looked larger than the one Peyton had. The realization knocked her hope down a peg. She decided to go ahead and try opening locker 202 anyway, just in case. The key wouldn't even go into the lock completely.

"Some of these locks get pretty sticky." The other woman spoke just before shutting her locker again. "I had to have my key replaced last week because it wouldn't open no matter what I tried."

Peyton jiggled the key one more time, then put it back in her pocket. "I may have to talk to them about this one, too." She gave a shrug. "Thanks."

"No problem."

Disappointed, she left the locker rooms and rejoined Jay outside. "Not here." She couldn't really have expected to find the right place at their first stop, but it would've been nice.

Neither of them spoke as they left the gym. The guy at the front counter didn't even seem to notice.

Back in the Jetta, Peyton pulled her seat belt across her body and clicked it into place. She reached for the notepad and put a big X next to Sal's Corner Gym.

One down.

Chapter Twenty-One

There was no doubt that Peyton was getting discouraged, and Jay couldn't blame her. He hadn't expected to figure out which lock the key belonged to right away, but to strike out completely was frustrating. Most of the lockers they'd checked out either had electronic passcodes or people brought their own padlocks to use. No lockers with the number 202 could be opened with the key Peyton had found.

Now, they'd reached the end of their list, and it was time to expand their search.

Peyton had her elbow resting on the car door, and her chin cupped in her hand, taking in the scenery as he drove back in the direction of the hotel.

He almost reached for her hand but stopped himself. It was frustrating how natural it'd been to hold her hand as they toured gyms this morning and how awkward it seemed now.

"Why don't we grab something for lunch, then head back to the hotel? We'll take another look at the map and wait for Nate to get back from his meeting." When she didn't answer, he nudged her arm with his elbow. "Peyton?"

Her head turned. "Hmm?"

He fought against the smile that tugged at the corners of his mouth and lost. "Lunch. What sounds good to you? We'll go through a drive-through and take it back to the hotel."

She sat up straighter and looked around. It solidified his impression a moment ago that she wasn't so much watching out the window as she was stuck in her own head.

"Do you still like Tex-Mex?"

"Honey, not that much has changed in two years." The term of endearment had already slipped out before he realized he was saying it. If she noticed, she didn't act like it.

"One of my favorite places isn't far. Go one more block, turn right, and it'll be on your right again."

Jay followed her directions. They both ordered a taco plate to go, and then he got back out on the street. "So if you ate here often, does that mean your apartment isn't far away?" He'd often wondered over the last two years where she lived and what her place looked like.

"We'll drive past the apartment building on the way back to the hotel if you turn left at the next light."

He did, and when she pointed out the apartment complex, he had to fight to keep from cringing. It was clearly rundown, and from the bars on the windows of nearby businesses, it wasn't in a great part of town.

"I know." Her voice was quiet. "It's safer than it looks, though."

The fact that someone broke in and ransacked the place said differently. He wanted to encourage her to live somewhere else if she moved back with Rosie once Trina's killers were caught, but he said nothing. If she couldn't afford it, there was only so much she really could do. The instinct to do something for her—to make sure she got into something better—was impossible to ignore.

She wouldn't welcome his help and now wasn't the time to push.

The Jetta's air conditioner took the amazing aroma of their food and distributed it throughout the interior. His stomach growled. It'd been a while since he'd had some good Tex-Mex.

He kept an eye on the road around them as they made their way back to the hotel. He hadn't seen any evidence of anyone following them, but he refused to relax completely.

Back at the hotel, they ate lunch and expanded their search to include twenty more possibilities while they waited for Nate to return.

Peyton never sat still for more than ten minutes before she was up again, walking around and glancing out the window. It was beginning to drive Jay crazy when Nate finally pulled up. Peyton met him at the door, opening it before he had a chance to knock.

"Sorry that took so long." He tossed his messenger bag on the small table near the door. "Patterson was late, then where we met was so loud, we couldn't talk about anything. So we got our food and had to relocate." He grabbed a bottle of water out of the cooler they'd brought with them from Destiny. "You guys find anything?"

Jay shook his head. "We visited every place on the list. The key didn't match any of the lockers." He glanced at Peyton. "No word yet from Logan. We were hoping you might've had better luck."

"Yes and no." He took a seat at the table and pulled his computer out of the bag as well as his tablet. He turned his attention to Peyton. "The good news is that the police aren't looking for you. At all. The same goes for Rosie. From what little information Patterson could gather, you are her only family. Jeb Carter was contacted. He wasn't interested in taking custody of his daughter. As far as everyone knows, it's assumed that you and Rosie left town to stay with family until the investigation is over."

The look on Peyton's face must have reflected the shock Jay felt himself. He shook his head. "There *is* no extended family. How on earth did the police reach that conclusion?"

"What about Trina? If I'm not a suspect, then what do they think happened to her?"

"That's where the bad news comes in. At this point, they feel it was a home invasion and robbery gone wrong with the suspects still at large." Nate tipped his chair back to balance on two legs. "Either this Detective Abbott has no clue what he's doing..."

"...or he's trying to sweep the whole case under the rug," Jay finished with a grunt. "Obviously, someone wants their money, and they're determined to threaten Peyton until they get it. If the police picked her up instead, it would limit their opportunities to do exactly that."

"Agreed." Nate's brows pinched together in anger. "The question is, is he coordinating directly with the killers, or is he simply a dirty cop who's accepting payment to make this happen? Either way, Patterson's working behind the scenes to get as much information as possible. He has to be careful who he questions and how he goes about it, though. If he gets shut down, then we won't have any connections to the PD. I feel like we're working in the dark already as it is."

"So what do we do next?" The question came from Peyton. "We can't check out every locker in town, and that's assuming we're even on the right track. If the police aren't looking for me, maybe I should go back to Trina's. Look around and see if she has some kind of safe or security box that hasn't been found yet."

That was the last place Jay wanted her to go. Not just because of the trauma she would have to face, but because it was the most likely place that Trina's killers would be waiting for her. "You're right. We may have to resort to that. But I don't think we're there yet. Let's keep looking at other options. Wait to hear from Logan. If we haven't found anything by tomorrow morning, we'll put that on the table."

Peyton didn't look convinced, but she didn't argue either.

Her phone pinged with a text. Her hand shook, and she took in a steadying breath before reading it aloud. "The clock is ticking."

Jay curled his hands into fists.

"I want to go by the restaurant where Trina worked." Peyton stood up and shoved her phone into the back pocket of her jeans. "If there are employee lockers, then our search might be over. I think it's a risk worth taking."

Chapter Twenty-Two

The sign for Down to Earth Eatery came into view. Peyton leaned forward to get a better look at the storefront while Nate chose a spot in the tiny parking lot. It was at least an hour before the dinner rush would begin. She couldn't imagine trying to get in and out while it was busy.

Jay scowled. "What kind of restaurant is this?"

Peyton might have laughed at his reaction if she weren't so nervous. Butterflies careened wildly in her stomach. "All vegan. All natural."

"No taste," Jay muttered.

Nate nodded from up front. "Amen."

She didn't disagree. Not that some vegan meals weren't good. But Trina had complained multiple times about how bland and gross the food was there. Peyton only stopped by the restaurant twice to visit her sister and eat lunch. She hadn't been overly impressed either time.

She released her seat belt and reached to open her door when Jay put a hand on her arm to stop her.

"We need to be cautious in here. Stick together. If there

are lockers, you're the only person they're going to allow access to them. If it weren't for that, I'd prefer that you stayed here in the truck and let Nate or me check it out."

"I need to be there. To see if I recognize any of the voices." She trembled at the thought of hearing either of the men again. If she did, it was essential that she not let on.

Peyton prayed that she'd be able to do just that.

Jay kept a palm against Peyton's back as they walked up to the door and went inside, with Nate coming in last. It took a moment for her eyes to adjust from the bright sunlight outside to the darker interior. There wasn't a lot of natural light coming in. It was a good thing the walls were painted a light gray, otherwise the dark wood of the tables and the counter at the front would have made the dining area too dim.

A woman was straightening things behind the front counter. She looked up when they entered and offered a friendly smile. "Hello, welcome to Down to Earth. Three for dining in?" She reached for a stack of menus.

The woman, whose name tag said Leslie, seemed so eager that Peyton almost felt bad they weren't going to be eating there. Almost.

"Actually, I was hoping to speak to your manager. My sister, Trina Kennedy, worked here."

The moment she said Trina's name, Leslie's face fell. "I heard about Trina. I can't even imagine... I'm so sorry for your loss. I've really missed seeing her around here." She clutched the three menus to her chest. "What can I do for you?"

"Thank you so much. It's been a shock." Peyton blinked back tears. How long would it be before she thought of her sister without wanting to cry? Right now, she couldn't imagine reaching that point. "I was wondering if Trina had left anything

135

personal here. If so, I'd like to pick it up. Do the employees have lockers or anything like that where they can store their things?"

Leslie looked like she wanted to help, but her expression turned guarded. "Like you mentioned, you should probably speak to my manager. She's also the owner. Just a sec, and I'll go let her know you're here."

With that, she hopped off the swivel chair she'd been perched on and headed for the back of the store.

As friendly as Leslie might have been when they first came in, the woman walking back with her was not. Leslie returned to her spot behind the counter and kept her head down.

The other woman, who looked to be in her fifties, approached them, back straight, and hands clasped in front of her. Her hair had been dyed an unnaturally dark color that made her face seem pale in comparison. "I'm Cindy Taylor. I own and manage this restaurant. I understand you're here inquiring about Trina Kennedy." Her voice was smooth with just the slightest hint of a Southern accent.

Peyton had the immediate impression of a teacher who was always disappointed in her students, no matter how hard they tried to please her. Trina complained about how Cindy hated it whenever Trina called in sick because it messed with the employee schedule. Now that she'd met her, Peyton could clearly see where that was possible.

She put a sad smile in place and extended her hand. "I'm Peyton Kennedy, Trina's sister."

Cindy shook it briefly. "I was horrified when I heard about what happened to Trina. I'm sorry for your loss." She sounded sincere, but her expression didn't match. Then again, she didn't have much of an expression at all.

"Thank you." Peyton motioned to Nate and Jay and

introduced them. "My friends have been helping me get some of Trina's affairs in order. It's been a rough few days." She didn't have to fake the way her voice caught.

Jay placed his hand on her lower back, and she leaned into the support. "I thought Trina said she kept a few things here. If so, I'd like to pick them up, please. Do you have employee lockers or anything like that?"

Peyton tried to act normal, even though her heart was pounding in her ears.

Cindy seemed to be contemplating the request. "I know this sounds insensitive, but one can never be too careful these days. Do you have some identification to prove you are who you say you are?"

"Of course." Peyton hadn't expected that at all. She got her wallet out and withdrew her driver's license.

Cindy studied it closely, compared the photo to Peyton, and finally handed it back with a firm nod. "She did leave a few things. If you'll follow me." She turned on her heel and led the way across the dining room.

Jay never let his hand drop from Peyton's back, and Nate quirked an eyebrow when he caught her gaze.

They entered the kitchen on the other side of the dining room. A man in a chef's uniform looked up from the counter where he was chopping something.

"Hello." Peyton hoped the chef might return the greeting.

Instead, Cindy spoke up. "This is my brother, Carl. He's been the chef here since we opened five years ago."

Carl only lifted his hand in response, which still gripped a large butcher knife, then returned to his work.

From there, they entered a cramped room that was set up as a lounge of sorts. There was a fridge on one wall, a small table with chairs, and a microwave resting on a rolling cart.

Cindy waved toward a bookshelf. "We don't have lockers, but every employee has a canvas cube they can use to store their things while they're working."

It took all of Peyton's concentration to hide her disappointment. She zeroed in on the canvas bins and spotted the one with Trina's name on it. She swallowed hard and reached for it. There was almost nothing inside and definitely no money.

She withdrew the blouse Trina must have brought in as a backup, a purple bracelet in the corner, and a tube of rose-scented lotion. Peyton had given Trina that bracelet last Christmas. She fingered it before slipping it into her pocket so she wouldn't lose it.

"Thank you." Her words were just above a whisper. She cleared her throat. "I appreciate you letting me come back here and pick these up."

Cindy stood at the entrance to the small space. "Not a problem at all. If you'll come this way, I'll show you to the front."

The chef was no longer in the kitchen on their way back through, but someone else was there stirring a large stock pot.

As soon as they were back at the main entrance, Cindy flashed a smile that was as fake as her hair color. "I'll be thinking of your family during this difficult time."

There was no doubt they were being dismissed.

"Thank you." Peyton mustered a weak smile, gave Leslie at the counter a small nod, and turned to leave.

Once outside, Nate grunted. "That was weird. Anyone else feel like that was weird?"

"Definitely." Jay opened the truck door for Peyton. "I

got the impression she didn't like you much. Although she had no desire to speak to Nate or me either."

Peyton shrugged. "Trina always said her boss was cold and unfriendly. I guess it wasn't an exaggeration. Maybe she's like that with everyone." She'd met people who felt that, since they were in a position of authority, everyone else owed them something.

Trina found it difficult to keep jobs for very long. This one, though, Peyton wouldn't have blamed her for quitting.

She just wished she could have heard the chef speak. Or the other guy who had been working in the kitchen when they left.

Chapter Twenty-Three

The rest of Sunday afternoon felt like it might drag into eternity. The one highlight was having the opportunity to talk to Megan after she called Jay on his cell phone. Peyton was relieved to hear that Rosie was doing well and seemed to have recovered from her cold. Megan assured her that she was enjoying the opportunity to cuddle with Rosie and that it was good practice for when their son was born.

While Peyton missed holding her niece, she was thankful that Rosie wasn't anywhere near Houston.

Right now, they were just waiting. Between the restaurant not having lockers and the fact that they hadn't heard back from Logan yet, Peyton was finding it difficult to stay positive.

There were less than twenty-four hours before the deadline, and she still had no idea where the money was or if it even existed in the first place. There was no telling if they knew she was back in Houston or not. Plus, she couldn't help but worry that both Jay and Nate were putting their lives on the line, too.

Peyton would never forgive herself if something happened to Jay because she dragged him into the middle of this.

She was supposed to be watching TV but truthfully had no idea what was on. The guys were playing a game of poker at the small table and using sugar packets for poker chips. They seemed evenly matched as the taller pile kept switching hands. She finally gave up on the TV and laughed as the two egged each other on.

Some of the jokes they told or teased each other about reminded her how much she had missed being away from Jay for two years. It felt more like two decades.

It was nearly seven when Nate's phone rang. He answered immediately, their poker game forgotten. "Hey, Patterson. What's going on?"

Jay glanced over at Peyton and gave her an encouraging nod.

They couldn't hear what the detective was saying on the other end, but it was clear Nate wasn't happy with it. "Like I said, without any other evidence or suspects, we're stuck up a creek without a paddle. We've got a timeline, and she needs to get into the victim's house. Of course not. She has a key." Nate looked to Peyton for confirmation. She gave him a thumbs-up, and he turned his attention back to the phone. His brows rose, and he lowered his chair to all four legs. "That would be great. Eight. Yep, we'll be there."

When he hung up, Nate glanced at his watch. "Patterson agreed to meet us at Trina's at eight so you can search the house."

Peyton should have been relieved at the thought of having another person there to watch for trouble while she went through the house. But Detective Patterson was a police officer. What if all of this was simply a trap to lure her into the open and arrest her?

Her thoughts must have been written all over her face because Nate quickly moved to reassure her. "Patterson's a good guy. I'd trust him with my life. He thinks if we go to the house at eight, it'll be late enough that most people are inside for the evening but light enough that having the lights on in the house won't draw too much attention. Not like they would in the middle of the night." He stood. "I'm going to run over to my room and change. I'll be back shortly."

Jay gathered the playing cards and slipped them back into the box. "What are you thinking?"

"That it feels like walking into a trap." Just saying the words made her stomach clench and her anxiety rise. "What if the guy who's sending me the texts is there waiting? What if Nate has it wrong, and Detective Patterson arrests me as soon as I show up?" What if everything went south, and Jay got hurt? She didn't say the last worry aloud.

Jay winced when he stood. "Nate and I will make sure you're okay." He set the cards on a nightstand and sat on the bed beside her. With one hand, he reached down and massaged his calf.

They'd done a lot of walking going in and out of so many businesses earlier. Of course, all of that had agitated his leg.

"Is it bad?" She angled her chin toward his leg so he'd know what she was referring to.

He shrugged. "It's annoying. But no, it's not bad." He straightened his leg and let it fall again.

"I'm glad." Peyton remembered the first time she'd seen his leg in the hospital and shuddered. "When someone called to tell me that you'd been injured by an IED ... I'm not sure I'd ever been so scared in my life. I mean, the possibility that something could happen to you while you were overseas was real, but getting that call... there's no way to prepare for that."

"I know. Same here." He swallowed hard and stared straight ahead. "I was part of a convoy heading back to base after—well, I'm still not allowed to give details of our mission. The vehicle in front of ours hit an IED. It took both of our vehicles out."

This was already more than he'd ever told her in the past. Peyton said nothing as she listened and prayed God would give him peace as he shared what happened to him. She tucked the hand closest to him beneath her thigh to keep from reaching out.

Jay scratched his goatee and then ran his hand through his hair. "When I came to..." He swallowed, his Adam's apple bobbing. "I'd been pinned under part of the truck. I couldn't free my leg, and the heat from the fires had turned the metal against my leg into a hot iron."

Peyton flinched at the visual. To think of Jay lying there, his leg burning, and being unable to escape was too much. She blinked back the tears that stung her eyes. "I can't even imagine."

"One of the guys was on fire less than three feet away. Victor. I couldn't get to him to help. I watched him burn to death right in front of me." He shook his head as though he hoped it might dislodge the memories. "For the longest time, I saw him die every time I closed my eyes. I still have that nightmare occasionally." He shifted closer to her and gently nudged her arm with his. "I'd give almost anything to take away the nightmares you're having. I know what that's like."

The tears she'd been fighting before won out, and a single drop escaped and made its way down her cheek. "I wish I'd known what you were going through. Maybe I could have helped. Or at least understood more."

He'd leave to go for walks in the middle of the night. Or get home super late and then crash. When he did wake up in distress, he'd push her away and leave the room. She hadn't known what to do and eventually stopped trying.

She regretted that. Maybe she should've gone on the walks with him. Or insisted he see a therapist. Anything to keep the chasm between them from growing wider.

"At the time, I didn't want you to know what I was going through. I already felt weak. I didn't want you to see me that way, too. I dealt with survivor's guilt, PTSD, and then the injury itself was incredibly painful. I was worried I wouldn't be able to fully use my leg again. I didn't want you to be stuck taking care of me."

"I knew you were hurting. I felt so helpless because nothing I did seemed to help. There was a lot of grief there, too. Because you might have come back, Jay, but you were never the same afterward. In a lot of ways, I felt like I'd lost you months before we decided to get a divorce."

It was one of the things she'd admitted in grief counseling. She mourned the loss of her marriage, but in reality, she'd felt like it'd ended long before it was official.

Maybe that's why she didn't fight against the idea of divorce as much as she should have. As much as she wished she had.

Jay's shoulders fell a little as though the weight of their decisions, of what they went through, were weighing them down.

Peyton slipped her hand out and placed it lightly on his knee. "I'm glad you found the support group and got the help you needed. I'm glad you gave yourself time to heal. What you did was really brave."

She didn't realize she'd been tracing a circle on his knee with one finger until he looked down at her hand. His gaze shifted to her face. The combination of regret and heat in his eyes sent her pulse thundering. Hope, fear, and uncertainty pushed her to her feet.

"Nate will be back soon. I should get ready to go." She turned away from him to retrieve her bag when Jay stopped her.

"Peyton?"

She heard him stand from the bed and then walk up behind her. Every cell in her body seemed attuned to him.

One breath. Two.

Peyton turned again and stepped into his arms. His palm was warm against her neck as his fingers threaded through her hair. When his lips found hers, she placed one hand against his chest just above his pounding heart and the other around his neck.

Oh, how she'd missed this. Missed *him*.

He cupped the back of her head and deepened the kiss. It reminded her of the thousands they'd shared before everything fell apart, and yet there was something different about it. Something new.

She melted against him moments before a knock at the door had them jumping away from each other.

Peyton rested her fingers against her lips as she tried to catch her breath.

"Hey, guys, it's Nate."

Jay's eyes slid closed, but not before she saw the heat in his gaze. The kiss had affected him just as much as it had her. The realization meant more than the kiss itself.

He opened his eyes again with a look of apology before going to open the door.

Nate stepped inside. "I figured we could take my truck.

I think it blends in a little better than the Jetta..." He paused and looked from Jay to Peyton, barely suppressing a smile. "And we're going to pretend like I didn't interrupt something here. Are you two ready to go? Patterson said he'll meet us there."

The exhilaration from the kiss gave way to a turbulent mix of fear and dread.

What if someone was waiting for them there? What if she couldn't find the money? Would the blood still be on the carpet? She pictured Trina on the floor, the crimson stain spreading.

"Hey." Jay's voice, along with a light touch to her shoulder, jolted her back to the hotel room. There was no missing the worry on his face or the flash of sympathy on Nate's.

She focused on the pressure of Jay's hand on her skin, trying to absorb every bit of his warmth and strength.

"You don't have to go. Nate or I can take the keys and see what we can find."

As much as she didn't want to go back, she knew she had to.

"I can do this." Her voice sounded more certain than she felt. She'd go back for Trina because she deserved justice and for Rosie because she deserved to grow up in a world where Peyton wasn't constantly watching over their shoulders.

Chapter Twenty-Four

J ay was still reeling from the kiss he'd shared with Peyton. Holding her in his arms had felt more than right. While she was there, he knew she was safe. Loved. Because he'd never stopped loving her, not even when things were at their worst between them. How could he have let her slip through his fingers? They should have tried harder. *He* should have tried harder.

But even as he thought about that, he knew he hadn't been in a healthy place to fix his marriage. He'd been an absolute mess, and it wasn't until he'd finally given it all over to God that he'd started walking the path to healing.

To think that Peyton had found God around the same time. Goosebumps peppered his skin at the timing of it all.

But what did that mean for them now? Was Peyton even meant to be in his future? The uncertainty ate at him. One thing was clear, though. He wasn't going to let her walk away without letting her know how he felt.

He'd chosen to sit in the back seat with her while Nate drove them to Trina's house. Jay wasn't sure he'd ever seen her this tense. Her hands were clasped in her lap, her left foot bouncing up and down, and her spine straight.

He reached over and took one of her hands. She threaded her fingers with his and squeezed. He'd do anything right now to spare her the nightmare of going back into her sister's house.

Nate glanced at them in the rearview mirror. "Father, we ask that You be with us as we head into a stressful situation tonight. Give us wisdom to help us locate what we need to find."

Jay nodded and continued the prayer. "We also ask that You cover Peyton with Your grace and peace. Help her to feel Your presence with each step she takes."

"Thank you, Father, for Your love and Your goodness," Nate continued. "Protect us. Keep us safe. In Your Son's name, we pray, Amen."

Jay and Peyton echoed the amen, and he squeezed her hand again. They rode the rest of the way to the house in near silence.

The first thing Jay noticed when they turned down her street was the police car parked at the curb.

"Looks like Patterson beat us here." Nate pulled up to the curb behind the other car. By the time he turned the engine off and got out, the officer was already approaching them. The men shook hands, and Nate motioned for Jay and Peyton to exit the car.

He made introductions. Officer Lee Patterson shook Jay's hand and focused on Peyton. "I'm sorry for your loss and everything you're going through."

"Thank you." Peyton's voice was barely above a whisper.

Jay put an arm around her shoulders, and she leaned into him. "I'd feel better if we got off the street and inside."

Patterson nodded. "Agreed. I understand you have a key?"

The question was directed at Peyton, who took her key ring from her pocket and held up a silver one. "Right here."

"Very well. Once you open the door, I'd like for you and Jay to stay just inside the house while Nate and I clear it. Understood?"

"Of course." Jay made eye contact with Nate, who nodded.

They'd spoken earlier while Peyton was in the bathroom. Nate would find a blanket and place it over the floor where Trina had been killed. There was no reason for Peyton to have to see the blood that likely hadn't been cleaned up yet.

Peyton unlocked the door and reached a hand in to turn the light on. Nate and Patterson went inside and began their search of the house. Jay followed Peyton, closed the door behind them, and locked it. She reached for his hand again and held it so tightly, that he feared the circulation might be cut off in his little finger. He rubbed the heart tattoo on her wrist with his other thumb.

He was relieved to discover that the placement of the couch prevented them from seeing the carpet where Trina had died, according to Peyton's descriptions.

It didn't take long for the other men to return. Nate laid a blanket on the floor, and Patterson returned his handgun to its holster. "We're all clear. I've got a mountain of paperwork to do. I'm going to sit in the car out front. If anyone is lurking around, I'll spot them. If I get called out, I'll be sure to let you know beforehand." He shook Nate's hand and then left.

Nate locked the door again behind him.

Peyton let go of Jay's hand and motioned toward the

149

hallway. "I think I should start in Trina's bedroom. If she was hiding money here, it makes sense she'd want to keep it close."

Jay agreed and intended to go along to help her search.

"Is there anywhere you want me to look?" Nate glanced around the large living room.

"If you could check the kitchen, that would be great. After that, feel free to search the living room." Peyton's frown intensified. "It'd be so much easier if we knew for sure what we were looking for." She sighed, and her shoulders tensed.

She kept her eyes straight ahead as they rounded the couch and stepped over the blanket on the floor. Jay's heart ached for her. She'd faced unexplainable trauma in this house and yet had returned to face it head-on, trying to find answers. To protect herself and her niece. His respect for her soared.

A chill settled as they continued down the hall and passed one room with a door that was only half on its hinges. A glance inside confirmed it was Rosie's room. This was where Peyton had made her desperate escape to get herself and the baby out of the house before Trina's killers kicked down the door. Jay could picture the scenario, and it made him furious that she even had to live through a situation like that. The fact that those people were still walking around terrorizing her was completely unacceptable.

The whole house left a heavy impression. Almost like how he'd expect a graveyard to feel in the middle of a stormy night. He didn't doubt that Nate and Patterson had done a thorough job of making sure there was no one else there with them. Even still, he was thankful for the gun nestled in its holster at his back.

"This one is Trina's. Was."

There was no emotion in Peyton's words as she led him into a large room. It'd been completely ransacked, similar to the pictures he'd seen of Peyton's apartment. If the killers, or unsubs, as Patterson was calling them, hadn't found what they were looking for, how was Peyton supposed to?

She went straight to the closet while Jay focused on the dresser. It felt wrong going through the deceased woman's things, but then again, most of it was strewn all over the floor already.

They searched as thoroughly as they could, leaving the immense amount of paperwork that had been knocked off the small desk in the corner for last. They considered not even looking at it except that it was impossible to tell if there was anything else underneath it all.

Peyton sifted through the loose papers quickly and tried to put them in a pile. "She was notorious for keeping every single receipt. Claimed the one time she didn't, she'd actually need it for a return." She shook her head, a sad smile on her face. "I used to tease her that, since she had so many and no orderly way to store them, she probably wouldn't be able to find it in her organized chaos anyway."

Jay didn't know what to say. He couldn't fathom having to go through his siblings' home and belongings like they were Trina's. Instead, he softly clasped her shoulder.

Twenty minutes later, they stood in the center of the room with nothing to show for their search aside from a photo album that Peyton clutched in her hands and a couple of pieces of jewelry she thought Rosie might want when she was older.

Jay had even gone so far as to look under the mattress, the bed itself, and checked for false bottoms in all the drawers. If Trina did hide something here, she'd done an excellent job of it.

They moved to the master bathroom and then on to the nursery while Nate went through the small guest room that seemed to serve as some kind of catch all for everything from craft supplies to crates of clothing.

Peyton stared at the crib, still clutching the photo album. "I should take some things back for Rosie." Her voice was heavy with emotion.

"I saw an empty box. I'll be right back." He returned moments later and set it on the floor. Peyton added the photo album and sniffed. "After everything is over, I don't know if I can come back into this house. Can you hire people to pack everything up and put it in a storage building?"

"Yes, there are companies who will do that for you." If she couldn't afford someone, Jay would set it up. Some day in the future, Peyton might want to go through everything, but he understood why it wasn't something she could do now.

She shook her head. "I thought, maybe I could come back here with Rosie. But there's no way. And my apartment isn't suitable for two people. I don't even have a job anymore." Her voice broke, and she bit her bottom lip to keep from crying. "What am I supposed to do now?"

Chapter Twenty-Five

Peyton had been doing such a good job of holding it all together. It'd taken everything in her to cross the threshold of the house and then to walk past the spot where Trina was killed. But standing in the nursery nearly did her in. Trina may have had many faults, and the house may have been a disaster, but she'd cared about her daughter. Rosie's room was decorated beautifully, and the little girl had everything she could have possibly needed.

Now Peyton would be the one responsible for making sure Rosie's needs were met and that she was well cared for. What if she wasn't up to the challenge? Not emotionally. No, Peyton loved her niece with all her heart. But financially. What if she couldn't provide health insurance or medication? What if she couldn't find a place to live that she could afford?

The weight of it all settled over her chest. She struggled to catch her breath, darkness crowding in until Jay's arms came around her.

"Breathe, honey. Breathe." He demonstrated with slow

inhales and exhales all the while rubbing her back in slow, calming circles.

She did her best to match his breathing until her heart rate slowed and the band around her lungs finally eased. Only then did she realize they were sitting on the floor, and she was leaning against Jay's strong chest. His hands were on her arms and his mouth near her ear as he murmured words of encouragement.

"Are you okay?"

She nodded. "Yeah. I think so." Peyton turned her head slightly to see his face. There was no judgment or impatience there. Only worry and compassion.

"You scared me. How long have you been having panic attacks like this?" He gently brushed some hair out of her eyes.

"The first one was in your office." She tried to smile but wasn't sure how successful she was. "I wonder if the fact that I've only ever had them in front of you means something significant."

He laughed, the sound vibrating against her back. "There's my girl."

He set his hands on her waist and helped her stand. When she turned to look at him, there was no hint of humor on his face. "You are *not* in this alone. I want you in my life again, Peyton. I don't know what that means yet or if we're even on the same page, but I need you to know that."

He left no opportunity for her to respond. He pressed a kiss to her forehead and moved away. "I'll check the closet."

He disappeared into the closet, and she just stood there, stunned by his words. He wanted her in his life again? Like, friends on social media who occasionally wished each other happy birthday? Or something more? The kiss they shared would suggest more, but they hadn't had a chance to talk about it, and everything between them was so complicated.

She got it, though. She couldn't fathom walking away after this and not seeing him again for another two years.

An hour later, it was nearly ten o'clock, and they were all still empty-handed. Peyton had filled the cardboard box with some of the special things that Trina had bought for Rosie along with some more clothing.

They met Nate in the hallway and were just about to trade rooms when Nate's phone rang.

"Hey, Logan." Nate listened for a moment. "Yep, let me put you on speaker. I'm here with Jay and Peyton."

A moment later, Logan's voice filled the hallway where they were all standing.

"Hey, guys. I'm sorry I couldn't get back to you sooner." Paper rustled in the background. "I don't think the key is going to belong to a gym. Most of them either have lockers with passcodes built in, or customers are expected to bring their own locks."

Peyton exchanged a look with Jay. They'd figured that out themselves, though there was no reason to tell Logan that.

"Any idea what kind of lock we might be looking for?" The question came from Nate. "We've been through the house once already. We're about to do a second sweep."

"There are no bus stations or subway lockers anywhere near your location. There's still a possibility it belongs to a bank safe deposit box. If that's the case, there's no way you're going to be able to access it. Not without a proper warrant. There *is* one more possibility, though. Peyton? Does your sister have mail delivered to the house? Or does her neighborhood have a community mailbox?"

Peyton shook her head, even though Logan wouldn't be able to see it through the phone. "It's delivered here to the house."

"Is there any chance she has a post office box?"

"I don't think so. She hated going to the post office. Whenever she had to mail something, she'd complain about the long lines she had to wait in just to buy stamps. Most of the time, if she did need to send something, she went to one of those little local places..."

Peyton stopped as her mind raced. There was something she'd seen back in Trina's room that was trying to work its way into her memory.

She jogged down the hall and went back to the piles of paper on the floor surrounding Trina's desk. The guys followed behind her. She knelt on the floor and started shuffling through the papers again.

"Hold on, Logan, Peyton may have something."

Jay joined her on the floor. "What are we looking for?"

"Receipts from one of those pack and ship places. I'm certain I saw several."

"That's great," Logan's voice filtered from the phone. "If you can figure out which one Trina frequented, she could've rented a box there. The mailboxes are open twenty-four hours a day. It'd be easy to swing by and see if the key opens one."

Peyton barely registered hearing Nate tell Logan he was going to hang up and help search and that he'd call him back. She wasn't even sure how long they were all going through paperwork before a logo caught her eye. She pulled that receipt out and held it up. "I've got it!"

Hope bloomed as she read the name aloud. "Cypress Avenue Pack and Ship. There are several receipts here."

She shuffled through them, announcing what each one

had been for. "Stamps. Mailing a box." Then one caught her eye. "And one for opening a large mailbox." She passed the receipt to Jay. "That's got to be it, right?" *Please, God, let this be right.*

Jay looked at the receipt and gave a nod. "It's the best lead we've had all day. Maybe she put the money there, figuring if she wasn't getting mail, it wouldn't be noticed for a while?"

"What's the date on that, Jay?"

"Less than two weeks ago." He told her the exact date.

Peyton looked through the receipts again. "This box was mailed on the same day. Maybe she sent it to someone else?" If that were the case, there was no way they'd be able to track it down before the deadline tomorrow.

"Or she mailed it to herself," Nate suggested. "I had an aunt who would do that with anything she deemed important. If that's what Trina did, it might have been placed in that mailbox and left there. Probably one of the safest places she could have stashed it outside of a bank."

Jay still held the receipt showing Trina had rented a mailbox. Peyton handed him the one for the package, too. He folded them, slipped them into a back pocket, and then extended a hand to help her up.

They made their way back to the front door, Jay stopping to pick up the cardboard box full of stuff, just as someone knocked on it. Nate looked through the peephole.

"It's Patterson." He unlocked the door, but the officer didn't come in.

"Hey, I've got a call out. There's a break-in in progress with shots fired a few streets over. Are you guys done?"

"We're on our way out." Nate waited until everyone was on the porch and then closed the door. Peyton locked it again.

"Keep me in the loop, Walker." Patterson used his radio. "This is Patterson. Show me en route."

With that, he jogged to his car and got in.

Jay placed a hand against Peyton's back as he looked up and down the street in front of the house. "We need to get out of here. Now. You still have the mailbox key?"

Peyton patted her pocket with a smile. "Right here."

Using his key fob to unlock the car, Nate waved them forward. "Let's go see if our theory is right."

Everyone was silent as Nate started the car.

Peyton stared through the window at the dark street outside. They'd made it in and out of Trina's house without incident. But somewhere out there were the men who had killed her sister. They expected Peyton to hand over a bunch of money tomorrow, and Nate had assured her that they would have a plan in place to catch whoever she was supposed to meet.

But what if it didn't work out? What if only one man showed up, and the other one got away with murder?

"Hey, guys. Even if we get the money tonight, I think we should go out and do some more investigating. Visit the grocery store where I worked. Maybe go back to the restaurant during the lunch rush. See if I can pick out the voices I heard that night. If we could get an ID on one or both of them, it can only help us."

Jay looked over at her. Even in the dark, there was no missing the concern on his face. "You have no idea what they look like, but I have no doubt they know who *you* are. It's risky."

She rested her arm against the window and turned to look outside again. There had to be another way. Maybe if Nate or Jay went in to talk to people and they used the phone or some kind of microphone. Then she could listen from—

Headlights blinded her as they barreled toward their truck.

Glass exploded all around her.

Everything went black.

Chapter Twenty-Six

There was no time between when Jay spotted the large service van barreling toward them and when it struck the driver's side of the truck. Peyton's scream pierced the air as windows shattered and glass rained everywhere.

The force of the impact sent the truck into a spin.

Jay was vaguely aware of Nate frantically trying to straighten their trajectory. Of Peyton's body moving like a rag doll.

With a sickening crunch, the truck hit a streetlight and came to a complete stop. Pain traveled into Jay's shoulders and neck.

The airbags up front deployed. Nate sagged and leaned against the airbag, unmoving.

"Nate!"

Smoke from the airbags filled the cab and made Jay's eyes water. He coughed and swung his attention to Peyton. Her chin touched her chest, and her hair hid her face from him. She wasn't moving.

"Peyton! Honey, can you hear me?"

He reached for her wrist, relieved beyond words when he felt her pulse. He needed to get her out of there and then check on Nate.

God, please let them be okay.

Jay moved to release his seat belt when the door next to Peyton jerked open.

A figure stooped at the entrance and leaned inside. There was just enough light from the streetlight to illuminate the large knife in the person's hand. He used it to cut Peyton's seat belt before grabbing her by the upper arm and dragging her out.

"No! Wait..." Jay scrambled to get to her side of the car when the figure stepped close again.

This time, Peyton was with him. She was clearly unconscious, and the person had a gun pressed to her temple. "Try anything, and she's dead."

Jay froze as he registered the unusually deep timbre of the man's voice. Was he the one Peyton had heard when Trina was killed? All Jay knew was that he had to stop the man from taking Peyton.

He slowly moved his hand toward the gun holstered at his lower back. Even if he could get to it fast enough, he didn't dare risk the other guy's gun going off and hitting Peyton.

The killer had the upper hand, and he knew it. With a deep laugh, he slowly backed away from the truck. His gun never wavered. Jay lost sight of Peyton as the forms receded into the darkness. He moved toward her door when a gunshot filled the air. The bullet hit the back of the seat beside him.

Jay ducked. When there were no other shots, he pulled his gun free and scrambled to the door. He got out just in time to see a dark vehicle pull away from the scene. It was too far away to read the license plate. Panic hit him square in the chest as he imagined Peyton in the hands of the man who'd killed her sister.

"No, no, no!"

He yanked his phone out of his back pocket and dialed 9-1-1. While it rang, he wrestled with Nate's door until he got it open enough to reach inside. Before he could check for a pulse, his friend groaned in response. *Thank God.*

"9-1-1. What is your emergency?"

"We were just run off the road, and my wife was taken at gunpoint." He was barely aware of the slip regarding Peyton. "Let Detective Lee Patterson know. We were just with him a few minutes ago." He leaned into the truck to check on Nate. The hair on the left side of his head was matted with blood. "We need an ambulance here."

Nate was breathing easily, and a quick check of his pulse told Jay that it was strong and steady. He had likely hit his head on the door when the initial impact took place. There was no way to know how bad the damage was yet, though. He took a handkerchief out of his back pocket and pressed it to the wound to try and stop the flow of blood.

The dispatcher assured him that help was on the way. She wanted him to stay on the line until emergency crews arrived, but he had another call to make.

Seconds later, Logan answered the phone. "Hey, did you guys end up finding anything?"

"Logan, listen to me." He recited their location. "Someone rammed Nate's truck and took Peyton. I couldn't see his face, and I couldn't get a plate. Can you check traffic cameras in the area?"

The sound of keys clacked in the background. "I'm on it. Are you and Nate okay?"

"Nate's hurt. I'm not sure how bad. They're sending an

ambulance now. I'm fine." Not completely true. He was already feeling the effects of the crash in the way his back and neck muscles were tightening up. His leg ached as well. But he could walk and function, and he wasn't going to stop until they'd found Peyton. "I asked for Detective Patterson."

"Good. If he can put in a formal request for my help, I can accomplish a whole lot more."

"I'll see what I can do." Logan was a master when it came to tracking people down. If there were enough cameras in the area, Logan might be able to tell where the car had taken Peyton.

"Jay? We're going to find her."

"I'm good." Nate shrugged off the EMT and got to his feet. "That'll do."

"We should transport you to the hospital for a CT scan to be certain you don't have a concussion or internal bleeding." The EMT didn't look at all happy to see Nate moving around.

Nate looked at Jay. "My friend here is a doctor. I'm good, right?"

The EMT had already cleaned and patched up the wound near Nate's hairline. The EMT was right, of course. Ideally, it'd be better for Nate to go to the hospital and make sure he didn't have a serious concussion. His reflexes were normal, as were his vision and balance. There was nothing that suggested they should be concerned. Besides, if their roles were reversed, they'd have to drag Jay to the hospital.

No doubt Nate was going to feel the effects of the accident tomorrow, but Jay was confident his friend was fine.

"I'll keep an eye on him. If anything changes, I'll take him to the hospital myself. We appreciate what you've done."

"Yes, we do." Nate reached out and shook the man's hand.

Detective Patterson pulled up then and jogged over. "You guys okay? I got here as fast as I could. The call-out earlier turned out to be fake." He looked over to where the white van and Nate's truck were. "I'm certain it's connected. I'm sorry. If I'd been following you guys, maybe they wouldn't have tried something this bold."

Nate clapped the man on the shoulder. "You were just doing your job. Listen, we figured out where Trina likely hid the money. If this guy gets the information out of Peyton..."

"Then that's where they'll be heading. What have you got?"

They told him about the key and the receipts from the shipping store.

Detective Patterson held up a finger, dialed a phone number, and made arrangements for someone to discreetly sit on the mailbox location until they had a plan in place. "Be aware that the suspect has a hostage, is armed, and should be considered dangerous."

Nate shook his head. "I didn't even see the van. If I had, maybe I could have done something to lessen the damage..."

"No. This isn't your fault. None of it."

There was no way Nate's truck was drivable. If Jay had to guess, it'd be totaled once insurance got a good look at it.

They needed to get a lift back to the hotel so they could grab the Jetta.

The thought of that man with his hands on Peyton made Jay's blood boil. His girl was a fighter, and right now, the guy needed her alive. All Jay knew was that they didn't have much time.

Chapter Twenty-Seven

A groan escaped Peyton's lips before she ever even tried to open her eyes. Her whole body hurt, right down to her wrists and ankles. Where was she? Her head pounded as she tried to go over everything she remembered.

They'd left the house and were on their way to check the mailbox Trina had rented.

The blinding headlights. The white van.

Her eyes flew open. The room didn't look familiar, and her heart pounded painfully. She took in the space around her. It was a dirty room with dingy lights hanging from the ceiling. What might have been windows looked like they were blocked with something to keep the light out. Or maybe to stop someone from leaving.

She was lying on her side on the concrete floor, and whatever was binding her wrists and ankles cut into them. She tried to twist her body and was finally able to see the zip ties that held her limbs in place.

Where was Jay? Was he okay? Nate? Had they survived the crash? Was Jay out there somewhere hurting and needing help? She looked around the room, but she was the only person there.

She had to get out. She needed to find Jay and make sure he and Nate were all right.

With some effort, she got herself into a seated position. She'd seen videos online of ways to break a zip tie. She tried to remember what the tricks were. She didn't even have time to formulate a plan before a voice spoke from a doorway across the room.

"Don't even think about it."

The man's deep, even voice washed over her like a bad dream. Memories from the night Trina was murdered swept in like a relentless flood. She gasped. "It was you at my sister's house."

The man laughed. "I thought you'd probably heard our voices that night. Trust me, I've been looking forward to meeting you in person for a while now."

With that, he left the shadows of the doorway and strode toward her, a sneer on his face. "It took some serious planning, but here you are."

"What about my friends? Are they okay?"

He shrugged. "I must admit that I have no idea whether they walked away from the accident or not."

Peyton refused to give him the satisfaction of falling apart. The van had hit the driver's side of the truck. If she was okay, surely Nate was, too. And Jay was on the other side of the truck. She refused to think any differently. The way she squared her shoulders must have told her captor everything he needed to know.

He shook his head pitifully as though he were looking down at a wounded puppy in the rain. "You Kennedy women are stubborn. Too stubborn for your own good.

You'd rather risk your life and those around you instead of simply handing over what wasn't yours in the first place."

He loomed over her now. When she tried to shift away, he backhanded her, sending her to the floor again.

Peyton's cheek stung, and blood trickled from the corner of her mouth. She refused to try and wipe it off on her shoulder. Instead, she maintained eye contact.

This guy was clearly one of those bullies who was going to say what he wanted to say—hoping she would counter him and give him a reason to lash out. She could tell by the way he was staring at her now, his eyes dilated, as though he were daring her to say something out of line. To challenge him.

Once he got what he wanted, he wouldn't hesitate to kill her.

Just like he killed Trina, of that, Peyton was certain.

"I want the money your sister stole. You found a key." He reached a hand into his pocket and produced the same key Peyton had found in the formula can. She could see the 202 etched into the side.

She suppressed a shiver at the realization that, while she'd been unconscious, he'd gone through the contents of her pockets.

"You came up empty-handed at your sister's house, didn't you? But I think you know where the money is." He waved the key in the air. "What does this key go to?"

When she didn't answer, he swept his leg back and kicked her in the side. The toe of his shoe dug into her ribs, sending pain radiating from her sternum all the way around to her back.

Peyton curled around the agony and tried to catch her breath. Her eyes watered.

Her captor chuckled. "I can do this all night. Where is my money?"

"I don't know for sure," she croaked. "Even if I did, why would I tell you? You're going to kill me no matter how this plays out."

The carefully controlled expression on his face didn't slip an inch. "You're not wrong. But what you can do is save the lives of the people you care about." He hiked an eyebrow. "I've done some research, my dear. Ex-husband Jay Baird. How nice that you've reconnected. It's a shame that it won't last. If he managed to survive the accident, he'll wish he hadn't by the time I'm done with him. Maybe I'll even bring him in so you can watch while I slowly end his life."

Peyton pushed the image he conjured from her mind. *Please let Jay still be alive, God. Please keep him safe.*

"Or how about that little brat? I'm assuming you found someone to care for her while you came back here." His mouth stretched into an evil smile. "I will search to the ends of the earth for her. Then I'll make sure she's reunited with her mother."

Rage flowed through Peyton, and it was all she could do to stay still. She'd caught her breath, and while her ribs still hurt, she thought she could kick out with both legs. But even if she managed to knock her captor down, how would she get away?

Until she could free her legs and attempt to escape, she needed to stay calm. Let him think he'd bested her, and maybe he'd let his guard down a little.

"Imagine what I'll do to both of them. Tell me what this key belongs to, or you won't have to imagine for much longer—" His phone rang then. He glanced at the screen, and a flash of annoyance crossed his face. "Don't get too comfortable."

With that, he flashed a toothy grin and turned on his heels to leave. He flicked off the light switch and closed the door behind him. A click suggested he'd locked her inside.

Peyton was bathed in darkness. The concrete floor beneath her suddenly seemed cold, and the air around her heavy. Goosebumps peppered her skin as she focused on the sliver of light coming from underneath the heavy door.

A sob caught in her throat.

There was no doubt in her mind that her captor would hunt them down. The idea of never seeing Jay or Rosie again on this earth was unthinkable.

No, she wouldn't allow them to be harmed. She might not have a choice but to tell her captor about the mailbox. But if she did, she needed to put off sharing that information for as long as possible.

Peyton struggled to a seated position. Her ribs protested, and the area where her hands and feet were bound together ached. She tried several of the suggestions she'd seen in a YouTube video for breaking out of zip ties, but they didn't work. As best as she could tell, her captor had used at least two for her hands and at least as many for her feet.

Without leverage, it would be nearly impossible to get out of them.

She had to go on the assumption that Jay and Nate were still alive. The alternative wasn't acceptable.

They were out there somewhere, and they were looking for her. They had to be.

"Please, God, keep them safe and help someone to find me. Please."

Chapter Twenty-Eight

J ay tossed two ibuprofen into his mouth and washed them down with gulps of cold water. He prayed they'd kick in soon and ease the pain in his neck. Whiplash was no joke, and if he thought he was uncomfortable now, experience told him it would only get worse over the next couple of days.

He handed two pills to Nate, who swallowed them dry. He glanced at his watch, then gave his phone an annoyed look.

They were sitting in the rental car, half a block from Cypress Avenue Pack and Ship, and waiting for a call from Logan.

As soon as they left the scene of the accident, they'd gone to the hotel. Nate quickly washed the blood out of his hair, then traded his soiled shirt for a clean one. Detective Patterson had taken their statements and gone to the precinct, promising to keep them apprised of the situation.

Jay had been unwilling to sit around the hotel room. They'd told Patterson where the money was likely being kept and that the man who took Peyton was going to get that information from her one way or another. Until the police had people in place to ensure the money wasn't removed from box 202 unless the suspect was apprehended, he wasn't taking his eyes off the building.

In the meantime, they needed a clue about who had taken her. They needed to find her before it was too late. Because if they'd been willing to kill Trina, they weren't going to just let Peyton go free once they found the money.

He pushed away the horrible thoughts that tried to enter his mind. Scenarios surrounding Peyton and where she might be right now. Was she frightened? Hurt?

He prayed for her safety and comfort.

Nate's phone lit up with an incoming call, and he answered it immediately. It was connected to the stereo system in the car so Jay could hear the conversation, too.

"Okay. I've officially been invited to the party by the Houston PD. I was able to locate video of the accident. You guys are lucky you even walked away from it." Logan cleared his throat. "We're looking for a 1996 Chevy Equinox. Either dark gray or black. I got a picture of the plates, but they came back as stolen. The plates are different, but there's a strong possibility that this is the same car Peyton saw outside Trina's house."

Nate nudged Jay and pointed out the window. "Hold on, Logan."

Jay spotted Detective Patterson coming their way. He jutted his chin toward the back door. Nate unlocked it, and the detective climbed in.

"I see you didn't stay at the hotel like I suggested." There was no surprise in his voice.

Jay ignored the comment. "Logan, Detective Patterson has joined us." He filled Patterson in on what Logan had told them so far.

Patterson got the license plate numbers and called them in. "I've got Detective Abbott on board. We're setting up a perimeter around the Pack and Ship. If someone tries to gain access to box 202, we'll be there to bring him in."

"What about Peyton?" Jay turned in his seat so he could see Patterson better. "There's no way this guy is going to send her inside to retrieve the money. They have to know we're watching for her. Once the suspect knows where it is, he won't have a use for her. We need to figure out where they are now and find her. Get to her before they get this far."

Nate gripped the steering wheel, his knuckles turning white. "Logan, were you able to use the cameras to track the car for any distance?"

"Unfortunately, not for long. It headed east for two blocks and turned right on Stepp Avenue. I lost it after that. I'm scanning camera footage for the same license plate, but if they've gone into hiding, we aren't going to have much luck."

"They may not even use the same vehicle when they come back to get the money. You never know, though. If this truly is the same car that was parked in front of Trina's house when she was killed... Most criminals aren't necessarily known for their intelligence." Patterson frowned. "Look, we're going to have this whole area covered. The best thing you can do is go back to the hotel—"

"Not going to happen." Jay shook his head. "The last thing we're doing is sitting around the hotel waiting for news. It wasn't a good look, but I'm the only one here who's actually seen the guy who kidnapped Peyton."

Patterson looked like he was going to argue until Nate agreed. "It doesn't hurt to have two more sets of eyes on the place."

"Fine." He pinned Nate with a glare. "But you stay in the car and call me immediately if you see someone you think looks suspicious. You are not to engage the suspect. Either of you. Understood?"

"Understood." Jay couldn't promise he'd follow the directive, though. Judging by the look Patterson gave him, the detective didn't think he would either.

"You have my number, Walker. Be safe. Logan, I'll be in touch." With that, Patterson got out of the car and shut the door behind him.

Logan's voice came over the speaker. "I'm sorry I haven't been more help. I'll keep monitoring video and let you know if anything comes up. Keep me updated, please."

"Thanks, man. Will do." Nate reached up and ended the call. He looked over at Jay. "What are you thinking?"

"That the kidnapper is too smart to come get the money in the middle of the night. He'll wait until tomorrow. Go in when there's a crowd. Try to blend in."

"It makes sense. I hope you're right."

"Yeah. Me, too." He just prayed the kidnapper had a reason to keep Peyton alive. Maybe the fact that no one was sure the money was even in the mailbox would be enough to make him hold onto her for a little longer.

Nate touched the bandage on his head and winced. "I knew how much the divorce affected you. How hurt you were. I don't know what I was expecting when I met Peyton, but she wasn't it." He seemed to consider his next words. "The two of you are good together, by the way."

"Yeah, we are." Emotion tightened Jay's chest. "I never stopped loving her. I just hope and pray I'll have the chance to tell her."

Chapter Twenty-Nine

It was impossible to know how much time had passed. Peyton drifted in and out of sleep. She didn't want to rest or let her guard down, but her body wasn't giving her much of a choice. It didn't help that it was so dark she had nothing to focus on.

The next time she woke up, it was because her arm had gone to sleep beneath her. She could barely feel her hands. Peyton made a point of moving them and flexing her fingers, then did the same thing with her toes. Every muscle in her body ached. She swallowed, and her dry throat protested. She didn't think she'd ever been this thirsty in her life.

She heard footsteps approach and forced herself to sit up. Pressing her lips together did little to stop her cry of pain.

The door opened, and light from the other side nearly blinded her. She blinked against it and tried to focus. The switch was flipped, and the room flooded with light. When she'd first awakened there, the overhead bulbs seemed dim. Now, they might as well have been spotlights.

Her captor approached with the confidence of a man who knew exactly what he was going to do next.

For the first time, Peyton wondered if the man had a day job. If he did, she imagined he was a stockbroker or maybe a car salesman. Someone who was good at pushing people to get what he wanted.

He stood in front of her, his arms resting at his sides. "Where's the money?"

The sound of shuffling drew Peyton's attention to the doorway. Another man stood listening in the shadows.

Her captor had said she was going to die no matter what happened. If that was the case, then she'd buy as much time as she could. Precious time for Nate and Jay to put a plan together to capture these guys so they never terrorized anyone again.

She sat up straighter and tried to ignore the pain in her ribs. "If I'm going to die no matter what, then I want to know where the money came from and how Trina got a hold of it in the first place." She coughed, and it made her throat ache.

That earned her a raised eyebrow. "That's not important. The thing you need to remember is that you can cooperate, and I'll leave your ex and the brat alone. Or you can refuse to tell me where the money is, and I'll make sure they die first, and then I'll move on to you."

She didn't doubt he was telling the truth. But as much as he wouldn't admit it, she held a degree of power over him, too. The question was how much. *God, give me the strength.*

"I may know where the money is." She swallowed, but it did nothing when her whole throat was so dry. She licked chapped lips. "Can I have some water?" Her voice croaked.

Her captor laughed. "I'm not wasting water on you

when your time is limited. Trust me, being thirsty is the least of your worries."

The man in the shadows left. When he returned a minute later, he had a bottle of water in one hand. "That's enough, Bull. Give the woman some water."

His voice slid through Peyton's memories like a snake. She shivered. This was the other man who had killed Trina. The one whose voice had sounded familiar.

He strode in, a bottle of water in his right hand. When he got close enough, he even looked familiar. But she still couldn't quite place him.

His eyes narrowed as he handed the bottle of water to his partner, the man he'd called Bull. "How do you expect her to tell you anything when she can barely speak?" With that, he retreated to the doorway.

If Bull was annoyed, he didn't show it. Instead, he unscrewed the lid and knelt in front of Peyton. He put the bottle to her lips and tipped it way up. Water cascaded into her mouth and overflowed to drip off her chin and onto the front of her shirt. "You're welcome," he said with a sneer.

Peyton flinched at the cold but swallowed several mouthfuls of water before Bull pulled the bottle away.

"That's enough. Think you can find your voice now?" He stood, put the lid back on the bottle, and tossed it to the ground between himself and the man in the doorway. "You were saying?"

She cleared her throat. At least most of the ache had eased. "I may know where the money is, but I haven't seen it personally." She pinned him with a glare. "And I won't say a thing until you tell me where it came from and how Trina ended up with it."

A muscle in Bull's jaw twitched as anger flashed in his eyes. Peyton wanted to look away, but she kept eye contact.

Refused to allow him to scare her into submission. She wouldn't give him the satisfaction.

He backhanded her, knocking her over onto her side. Tears sprang to her eyes while the taste of blood coated her tongue. She pushed herself back up again.

Bull didn't seem phased. "Not the sharpest knife in the drawer. Then again, neither was your sister. She got nosy and found out that not all businesses operate strictly to make a living. Some specialize in hiding the source of their funds."

"Money laundering." Peyton spat out the words.

Trina probably had no idea about the restaurant's illegal activity when she first started working there. Considering everything she knew about the place, this made a lot of sense. A realization struck her. She swung her attention to the man in the doorway. It was the chef from the restaurant.

He'd sounded familiar because one of the two times she'd gone to the restaurant to say hello to Trina, he had gotten into a debate with one of the customers over how something was prepared. She'd glanced at them but had made a point of not staring, which was why she wasn't sure who he was when she saw him at the restaurant this last time.

The chef, who she remembered Cindy introducing as Carl something... Tyler or Taylor, stepped into the room. He didn't look overly happy that Peyton knew who he was.

"Trina should have been thankful for a job. Stayed in her lane." The frown lines at the corners of his mouth deepened. "Instead, she stole a quarter of a million dollars."

Peyton's eyes widened. She'd had no idea there was that much money at stake. Could a quarter of a million dollars fit in a cardboard box small enough to be stashed in a mailbox? "So, who's the brains of your operation? You or your sister?"

Carl gave Bull a sharp nod, and he immediately struck her for her question. This time, black spots floated in front of her eyes as she tried to push herself to a seated position again. A tear slipped down her cheek.

Had Trina been trying to shut down the operation? If that was the case, wouldn't she have gone to the police? She might still be here today if she had. Or had she really flat-out stolen the money and hoped to get away with it?

Peyton shook her head and tried to clear the cobwebs that threatened to muddy her thoughts. "It doesn't make sense. Why would she steal your money?"

Trina had to know they'd come after her. Once she realized they knew she'd taken it, why didn't she just give it back? At that moment, Peyton had to suppress a surge of anger toward her sister. Trina could've come to her. If there had been a problem, they could've worked together to find a solution.

Bull shrugged. "Desperate people do stupid things."

That still didn't explain why Trina would've taken the money.

"You killed Stephen Lewis. Why?"

If her captor was surprised that she knew, he didn't show it. If anything, he stood straighter. "You'd be surprised how many secrets are whispered in the bedroom."

He winked at Peyton, and her skin crawled.

The blood on her face was drying, and the sensation made her itchy. She rubbed her chin on the sleeve of her shirt. "Except in this case, because if he'd told you what you wanted to know, then I wouldn't be here." She raised her brows, daring him to contradict her.

His eyes narrowed. "He seemed to believe that the money was stolen for him, but he hadn't yet received it. He suggested that you might know where it was. Told me about

Destiny and your ex-husband. See, there was plenty of pillow talk worth mentioning."

The irritation moments earlier disappeared. Instead, there was excitement in his eyes. This was a guy who clearly loved his job.

Carl stepped forward. "Enough! Stop playing around. Get the information we need and get rid of her." With that, he turned and left the room. A few minutes later, Peyton heard the sound of a vehicle starting up outside.

She tamped down the panic that rose at the realization that she was now alone with Bull. While Carl didn't seem to care whether she died, she didn't think he'd prolong her suffering. Bull, on the other hand, clearly enjoyed this entire process way too much.

As though he could read her thoughts, Bull shook his head in mock sadness. "He's a man who can't appreciate the art of interrogation." He crouched down so he was eye-to-eye with Peyton. "Tell me where the money is. Tell me now, or I'll beat you within an inch of your life, and then make sure you stick around long enough to watch me kill your ex and the kid."

Chapter Thirty

It took everything in Peyton not to look away from Bull's intense stare. He was not only sure of himself, but he was enjoying every minute of her discomfort. Not just the physical but her mental anguish. He wanted her to be afraid for her life.

And she was. She didn't want to die, but she was even more worried about something happening to Jay and Rosie.

As much as she wanted to keep the money out of Bull's hands, she needed to make sure the people she cared about were safe.

Peyton's eyes narrowed. "How do I know you won't kill them anyway?"

A hint of irritation sparked in Bull's eyes before he pulled his usual composure back into place. He chuckled, although it sounded forced. "As long as you tell me where it is, then they'll be safe. I was hired to find the money. Once I do, I'll get my payment, and I couldn't care less about them. I had no intention of killing your sister either. If she'd just handed over the money, she could have walked away."

Peyton had literally no reason to believe him. For all she

181

knew, he would go on a killing spree as soon as he had his hands on the money. She pressed her lips together, wishing she knew what to do.

Bull stood to his full height, anger contorting his face into something that made her flinch. He reached down, grabbed her by the hair, and used it to yank her to her feet.

Peyton's scalp stung as though it were burning. Her feet, which hadn't moved freely in way too long, sent shooting pain up her shins as she tried to get her balance. Tears blinded her.

His other hand grasped her throat and squeezed.

"Your ex and that friend of yours were at Trina's house tonight. I'm willing to bet they know where the money is, too. Maybe I should end you now and see if they're any easier to work with."

Peyton gave a barely perceptible shake of her head.

He released her throat.

She gasped, and sweet oxygen traveled to her lungs, triggering another round of coughing.

Bull's lips curled in disgust, and he let go of her hair.

With a groan, Peyton slumped to the ground. Her eyes slid closed as she tried to steady her breathing.

Her captor towered over her. "You have one minute to start talking."

She struggled to swallow. It was difficult enough before with a parched throat. After he choked her, it felt as though the tissues themselves were swollen.

"Trina rented a mailbox at one of those Pack and Ship places. That same day, she mailed a box to herself. I think the key is what opens the mailbox and that the box probably has the money in it."

"Which place?"

"It's not far from Trina's apartment." There was no way

she was going to tell him everything. If she did, he'd just kill her before leaving to retrieve the box. Or if he did leave her alive, it was highly unlikely anyone else would be able to find her here. She lifted her chin. "I'll tell you once we're both in the car."

The anger on his face eased a little, and he studied her. "It wouldn't hurt to have some leverage in case your friends get there first. We'll go in the morning and pick up the box. It's always busy right before everyone goes to work. It'll be easier to get in and out without anyone noticing."

"What if the police are there? What if your buddy who just left gets to the box first and leaves you high and dry?" She threw out every question she could think of, desperate not to spend the night tied up on the cold, hard ground. The sooner they made their move, the sooner the police could apprehend him. At least, that's the outcome she was praying for.

He shifted his stance, his body radiating confidence. "Thankfully, he's got a buddy in the police department. I'm not worried about them interfering." He jabbed a finger in her face. "You'd just better hope the money's in there."

Chapter Thirty-One

Sleep had been elusive for the most part. Nate and Jay had agreed to take turns trying to get some rest while the other kept an eye on Cypress Avenue Pack and Ship. According to Patterson, there were officers out there watching the business, too, which was just fine. Another set of eyes or two certainly didn't hurt.

Every time Jay fell asleep, he dreamed about Peyton being held against her will. He prayed she was still alive. That her captor would keep her around until they could find a way to get her to safety.

Patterson said he'd come back by to inform them of the official plan.

Until then, they were stuck in the Jetta while a knot the size of Texas grew in Jay's stomach.

"As soon as the coffee shop opens, I'll run in and grab us breakfast. And use the bathroom." Nate looked longingly at the dark storefront.

Jay sympathized. He could use a restroom, too. And as much as he didn't want to eat, food would settle his stomach. Make it easier to focus. He wanted to be clearheaded and at his best when someone showed up for that box.

Sitting around and simply waiting was one of the most difficult things he'd ever had to do. Every time he started to get anxious or worry about Peyton, he prayed for her. He had no idea how many times he'd prayed—he'd lost count long ago.

One thing he hadn't been good about since becoming a Christian was memorizing Bible verses. He'd already promised God that would change once this was all over.

A couple of Sundays ago, the pastor had spoken about praying in all situations. Suddenly, one of the verses he spoke about came to mind. Something somewhere in Thessalonians about being thankful in all things and praying without ceasing. The pastor had talked about not being anxious but giving every worry to God.

That's what he was trying to do, and it took regularly handing Peyton and her situation to Him. Jay was thankful they weren't going through this alone. Nate, Logan, and Patterson had their backs. Along with the rest of the police officers who were hopefully putting together a plan to not only find Peyton, but also arrest everyone involved.

It was just after four in the morning when they spotted Patterson jogging down the street in the dark. He rapped on Nate's window. Nate unlocked the Jetta's doors, and Patterson slipped inside.

"All right. We've contacted the manager of the business. As soon as they're open, one of our guys will be stationed inside behind the counter as an employee. We'll have two other people on the street outside blending in. Everyone knows which mailbox this guy's going to check, so if anyone so much as looks at box 202, we'll be right there waiting."

He leaned forward and put a forearm on the backs of

each of their seats. "The two of you are to remain here. Do not get involved." He handed Nate a radio. "You can reach me with that. If you see Peyton or anyone you recognize, let me know immediately. Otherwise, stay off the radio."

Nate nodded. "You got it."

"I'm serious. Abbott's not at all happy about the joint investigation. He tried to get me pulled off, but his boss overrode him. We may only have one shot at this. We need to make it count."

The knot in Jay's stomach tightened. "All we want is to get Peyton back safely and to catch the men who killed her sister."

"Then we're on the same page. I'll keep you in the loop."

With that, Patterson got out and disappeared into the darkness.

Jay was all for playing by the rules. But if it looked like Peyton was in trouble at any point, her safety was his priority.

Chapter Thirty-Two

Peyton shivered uncontrollably. She wasn't sure if the room was really that cold or if some of her injuries were more severe than she thought they were. Breathing deeply hurt, and her head throbbed mercilessly. The headache was likely a result of dehydration. She worried that the pain while breathing was due to a bruised or broken rib. With her feet still bound together and her hands zip-tied behind her, she couldn't even check to see how tender the area was.

Her thoughts shifted to Jay. Everything in her assured her that not only was he alive, but he and Nate were staking out the Pack and Ship building. Was Patterson there, too? Did they have a big, elaborate plan in place to catch Bull when he showed up to retrieve the box?

But what about Carl? Or the connection he had with the police department? What if that person was working with Nate and Jay right now?

Bile rose in her throat. She wanted to escape and warn them, but every attempt to free her limbs only resulted in more pain as the plastic cut into her skin.

She finally allowed herself to lean against a wall and close her eyes as she sent up a silent prayer. *God, You know the situation we're in, and I'm confident that only You can get us out of this mess. Please give Jay, Nate, and the police the wisdom to know what to do. Please protect Jay, Nate, Patterson, and everyone else who is putting their lives on the line to end this nightmare.* She took in a slow, painful breath. *Please protect me, too. I have a hard time believing Jay and I have been given this chance to reconnect, only to have it all be taken away. Thank You for always being there for us.*

She whispered an amen.

With no way to tell how much time had passed since Bull had been there, the minutes seemed to drag.

Finally, when she didn't think she could stand it anymore, the door opened again, and Bull strode inside. "It's time for our little road trip." He knelt and took a knife from his belt. "I'm going to free your legs. If you try anything, I'll bury this knife in your heart. Do you understand?"

Peyton nodded, her eyes wide.

He all but dragged her out of the room, through a dingy house that had clearly seen better days, and out the front door.

Peyton tried to get her feet underneath her and stand on her own, but her ankles throbbed as circulation slowly flowed back to her feet.

It was just getting light enough to see the gravel driveway out front. She didn't recognize their location at all.

There were at least five vehicles that she could see parked along the driveway.

Bull popped the trunk of an old, olive-green Honda Civic.

He was going to put her in the trunk!

He stopped at the trunk and turned to reach for her. That's when she threw her shoulder into him and pivoted in the opposite direction.

She only got a dozen steps away before she was knocked to the ground. She rolled to her back to find him standing over her, fury blazing in his eyes.

"If I didn't still need you for my backup plan, you'd be dead right now." He reached into his back pocket and withdrew a zip tie. Ruthlessly, he put it around her ankles and yanked it tight. He stood and dragged her toward the car. With a grunt, he picked her up and dropped her into the trunk.

"Where is the mailbox?"

"Cypress Avenue Pack and Ship. Mailbox 202."

Without hesitation, he grabbed a roll of tape, ripped off a piece, and put it over her mouth. He grinned down at her. "That's better."

He slammed the trunk closed.

The stuffiness stole her breath, and the darkness closed in around her. But it was the tape over her mouth that kicked her panic into high gear.

Peyton's breaths came faster until suddenly she could hear Jay's voice in her head.

Breathe, honey, breathe.

She imagined he was holding her in his strong arms. Slowly, one breath at a time, she took precious air in through her nose and focused on the way her lungs expanded, then emptied. Over and over again.

The car rumbled to life.

Peyton had no way of knowing how far they were from the Pack and Ship. She got the impression that Bull was working on his own, though. At least for this part. Which meant he was likely going to leave her locked in the trunk until he got what he wanted.

If he succeeded in getting the money, he'd take her somewhere, kill her, and likely dump her body. If he didn't find the cash and made it back to the car, he might kill her out of spite. If the cops caught him while he was trying to get the box, they would have no idea she was in the trunk. She could die from the heat or dehydration.

She absolutely needed to free herself or at least find a way to let people know she was in the car. But she couldn't do anything until she freed her hands.

When Bull tossed her into the trunk, she'd landed with her hands facing the back of the car. Methodically, she felt around the area until her hand touched some kind of hook. Maybe a cargo hook? She felt for the edge, and managed to wedge it beneath the double zip ties around her wrist. It caused the plastic to dig into her skin even more, but she tried to picture Rosie's sweet little face. With a cringe, she yanked hard away from the hook.

The zip ties snapped, but not before they cut into her skin. Thanks to the tape over her mouth, her cries of pain were muffled. For the first time in hours, she moved her hands in front of her. Her shoulders screamed in protest.

As fast as she could, she found the edge of the tape and ripped it off her mouth. She took a moment to breathe and calm herself. She needed to think. It was difficult when she couldn't see a thing. Was there a crowbar or something else she could use to defend herself?

She patted around the trunk but found nothing.

In her trunk, there was an emergency release. She felt along the edge and top of the trunk but couldn't find one. It was an older car. Maybe they didn't have releases when this car was made. She wasn't sure, but she couldn't keep searching for something that might not be there.

She needed to find a way to let someone know she was in the car.

Peyton vaguely remembered watching a show where someone had managed to kick out a brake light and stick her hand out to wave down help. Was that even doable?

With a groan, she bent at the waist and reached toward her feet. She needed to get the zip tie off. Thankfully, Bull only used one this time. If she could just figure out how to snap it...

She got four fingers between the zip tie and her shins, took a deep breath, and yanked it with all her might. She lost her grip, and her feet hit the wall of the trunk.

Peyton held her breath and prayed her captor hadn't heard the noise as well. It took two more tries before the tie broke, and if she hadn't been lying down, she might have fallen backward.

This was better. At the very least, she had the chance to fight back the next time he opened the trunk. No matter what happened, she wasn't going down without a fight.

Chapter Thirty-Three

J ay finished his small cup of coffee and absently set it into the cup holder in the console. It was nearly eight in the morning, and the whole street was bustling. The little coffee shop had a constant turnover of customers as people grabbed breakfast or a pick-me-up on their way to work.

The Cypress Avenue Pack and Ship was supposed to open at eight as well. Already, there were three customers lined up at the door waiting to get in. None of them looked familiar, and Jay had a hard time believing their suspect would be standing in full view like that. No, he'd wait until this initial rush was over and just go in and out with the other customers.

Nate scanned the street, radio in hand. "There are too many vehicles coming and going," he mumbled.

Jay wished he'd gotten a better look at the guy when he'd taken Peyton. They might not even know it was him until he tried to get into mailbox 202. Or it might not even be the same guy.

He took in one side of the street all the way up past the

Pack and Ship and then across the street and back. He skipped over the coffee shop and then stopped. One of the men at a table outside caught his eye, and he leaned forward to get a better look.

Nate was instantly on alert. "What is it?"

"See that guy in front of the coffee shop? Third table from the right with the large coffee."

It took a second, but then Nate zeroed in on him, too. "I think that's..."

"The chef from the restaurant." Jay nodded. "I think so, too." He glanced at Nate. "What are the odds it's a coincidence?"

"Well, we're not leaving anything to chance." He activated the radio. "This is Walker."

"Patterson here. What have you got?"

Nate gave a description of the man and let Patterson know who he was. "It might not mean anything. But Trina worked at that restaurant. His sister, the owner, was incredibly unfriendly and cold. I find it odd that he happens to be sitting outside, just a few doors down from the Pack and Ship today."

"Agreed." A moment of silence. "Abbott's putting a man on him. Patterson out."

A large van vacated a parking spot between the coffee shop and the Pack and Ship. A moment later, an ugly green Honda Civic pulled in. Unlike most of the other patrons who seemed in a rush to exit their vehicles and get in line for a coffee or pastry, this person sat in the car for several minutes.

Finally, an average-sized man stepped out. He started walking toward the Pack and Ship, his gaze straight ahead, like a man on a mission.

Jay glanced at the chef and noticed that, even though he

was still nursing his coffee, he'd sat up straighter and was watching the other man as well. "You see the guy who just arrived in the Civic?"

"Yep. He isn't quite blending in, is he?"

"Nope, and the chef is watching him, too."

Nate verified it for himself with a nod. "Calling it in." Into the radio he said, "This is Walker. You've got a man headed your way. Dark jeans, blue shirt, short hair, average height. Our friend at the coffee shop is watching him. This may be our guy."

"Stand by."

The silence was deafening as Jay and Nate watched the man walk into the Pack and Ship and disappear from view.

Patterson's voice came over the radio. "The suspect has a key and is approaching the row with mailbox 202. He's opened the door and is retrieving the box." In the background, they heard, "Move in! Move in!"

Jay waited on the edge of his seat until the Pack and Ship door opened again. Patterson emerged along with another officer, the suspect between them. His hands were secured with cuffs behind his back.

Unable to wait any longer, Jay got out of the car, slammed the door behind him, and jogged across the street.

As he approached, the man looked anything but defeated. He grinned, the smile stretching the corners of his mouth while his eyes remained cold.

"Ah. If it isn't the ex."

It took everything in Jay not to slam a fist into the man's face. "Where is she? Where's Peyton?"

"My condolences." His grin didn't waver.

Suddenly, Nate was there, a firm hand on Jay's shoulder.

Before Jay could do anything, a gunshot rang out. A woman screamed, and people scattered in confusion.

Jay spun around. Where had the shot come from? He didn't see anyone with a gun, but the chef was no longer at the table in front of the coffee shop.

Patterson spoke into his radio. "Shots fired! Shots fired! Suspect has been hit."

No!

The suspect slumped forward. The officers held onto his arms, keeping him from falling. Blood dripped onto the pavement at his feet. They eased him down and turned him over, but the man's unseeing eyes and the bullet wound to his chest left no doubt that he was already gone.

Jay's heart plummeted. He refused to believe that Peyton was dead, but how were they going to find her now?

Another voice came over the radio. "Second suspect seen running from the crowd with a firearm. We are in pursuit."

Everyone remained cautious as Patterson spoke into his radio. "The original suspect is down. We're going to need an ambulance at our location. Patient will be DOA." Another few moments of silence. Then he spoke again. "Abbott, have you located the shooter?"

"Negative. The shooter is in the wind. I'm on my way back."

Jay stared at the dead man, a chill racing through him. The sounds around him faded until one voice seemed to work its way through everything else.

"Help!"

He blinked and held his breath. Had he really heard that voice?

"Help me!"

Nate's head lifted, and he scanned the crowd.

Jay turned and looked down the street behind him. "I heard it, too." It was Peyton. He was sure of it. His gaze settled on the green car their dead suspect had arrived in earlier, and he took off at a jog. "Peyton!"

"Jay? Jay!"

He rounded the car, Nate on his heels. One of the brake lights had been knocked out, the red shards scattered on the pavement. A single hand reached through the narrow space, blood covering her wrist and dripping down her fingers.

"Nate! She's in the trunk."

"I've got it." He took a tool out of his pocket and used it to shatter the window so he could open the door and pop the trunk.

Jay lifted it to find Peyton curled inside. Her face was dirty and streaked with dried blood. Blood marred the skin on each of her wrists and her ankles and feet as well. Her lip was split and puffy. He tried to catalog her wounds as he gingerly lifted her out of the trunk.

Her arms went around his neck as a sob shook her body.

Patterson spoke from somewhere behind him. "We're going to need another ambulance immediately. We've got a female, thirties, multiple injuries."

"I've got you." Jay was afraid he was going to hurt her, but if anything was causing her pain right now, she didn't seem to notice. "You're safe. Thank You, God. Thank You for saving her."

"Kicking out the taillight was genius." Nate reached out and put a hand on her shoulder. "That probably saved your life."

Jay glanced at the trunk and saw the broken zip ties. The monster had tied her up in there. If they hadn't found her, she could have died from heat exposure when it warmed up later. He buried his face in her neck. "I was so scared I'd never see you again."

She nodded. "Me, too." She lifted her head and swiped at the tears on her face. The combination of tears and blood left stains on his shirt.

Sirens announced the presence of an ambulance as it made its way down the street toward their location. Two EMTs unloaded a gurney and jogged over. A tall man with sandy brown hair gave her a gentle smile as Jay placed her on the gurney. She cried out in pain. The sound nearly tore his heart in two.

The EMT stepped forward. "I'm Curtis. Can you tell me your name?"

"Peyton. Peyton Kennedy." Her voice sounded hoarse, and she coughed. "I'm so thirsty."

Curtis nodded toward the other EMT, who retrieved a bottle of water from the ambulance. Curtis took it from him, opened the lid, and handed it to Peyton. "Take slow sips at first. We're going to take good care of you."

Jay watched as she took several swallows, her eyes sliding closed with relief.

Curtis placed a kind hand on her arm. "I need you to tell us where you hurt the most."

Peyton handed the bottle of water to Jay. Then, she gingerly touched her left side. Jay reached for her hand.

"I'm going to take a look, okay?" Curtis lifted her shirt to reveal a dark bruise forming across her ribs.

There was no doubt she'd been kicked. Anger like Jay had never known before surged through him. If the man who had taken her wasn't dead already, Jay would have taken care of the job himself.

Curtis didn't hesitate. "We need to get her to the

hospital and get some x-rays. We may be looking at broken ribs." He glanced up at Jay. "Are you riding with us?"

"Yes." Jay looked at Nate.

"Go. I'll meet you there."

Jay nodded his agreement. He didn't want to let Peyton out of his sight.

Patterson walked up and gave her a kind smile. "You are one of the strongest people I've ever met. I'm glad you're okay, Peyton."

She smiled weakly in return.

They'd nearly wheeled her to the ambulance when she grabbed Jay's arm and squeezed. "Wait! The other man. It's Carl Taylor. From the restaurant."

"We know, honey. He shot and killed the man who kidnapped you. The police are trying to find him now." He pressed a kiss to the back of her hand.

Her eyes widened, and she looked around them as though she was afraid. "It's not just him. The restaurant has been laundering money, and Carl has a contact in the police department who's making sure everything stays under the radar." She coughed again, and her eyes watered.

"We need to get going," Curtis insisted.

Jay exchanged looks with Nate and Patterson.

Patterson seemed conflicted as he scanned the officers around them. "Has anyone seen Detective Abbott?"

An officer nearby nodded toward the coffee shop. "He went that way maybe two minutes ago."

Curtis and the other EMT carefully lifted Peyton's gurney into the ambulance. Jay followed. Before the ambulance doors closed, he heard Patterson speak into his radio.

"Detective Abbott. Report in immediately." When there was no response, Patterson said, "I want Abbott found now."

The doors closed, blocking all sounds from outside.

Jay reclaimed Peyton's hand and brushed some of her hair out of her eyes. "I'm sorry we didn't find you sooner. I'm so sorry this happened to you." He pressed a kiss to her forehead as tears pricked his eyes.

"It's okay," she croaked. "I didn't know what happened to you after the accident, but I refused to believe you'd been killed. I knew you were out there looking for me."

She smiled at him. It was a little wobbly, and she looked exhausted, but there was no missing the sincerity in her eyes.

"I never would have stopped searching for you."

Chapter Thirty-Four

Peyton wasn't sure what kind of pain medication the hospital had given her once she arrived, but she was thankful for it. By the time the ambulance got her to the emergency room, she was in so much pain it was all she could do to stay awake.

Two hours later, she was resting as comfortably as possible. She had three severely bruised ribs, contusions on her face, and wounds on her wrists and ankles thanks to the zip ties. The doctors said she was also severely dehydrated.

All Peyton knew was that she was so exhausted she could barely keep her eyes open. Jay's face, and the feel of her hand in his, were the last things she registered before sleep finally claimed her.

The next time she woke up, she felt disoriented. The ER room was dimly lit, and the beeping of the monitors in her room competed with those beeping down the hall. She looked to her left to find Jay sitting in a rather uncomfortable-looking chair. His eyes were closed. As though he could sense she was awake, his eyelids lifted. He sat up straight and leaned forward to cover her hand with his.

"Hey, you. How are you feeling?"

"Better knowing you're here." She wasn't feeling nearly as lightheaded or thirsty either. But mostly, she was relieved to finally feel safe. "How long was I asleep?"

Jay glanced at his watch. "Almost two hours."

"Wow."

He gently ran a finger over the bandage on her wrist. "They aren't planning to admit you, but they wanted to make sure you are properly hydrated and not feeling dizzy before they let you leave."

Peyton imagined the damage the zip ties might have done to her wrists. "What did the doctor say?"

He leaned forward and pressed a kiss to her cheek. "He said you'll make a full recovery, but you're going to be mighty sore for a while." He brushed the hair off her forehead. "I need you to promise me that you're going to take it easy. Make sure you allow your body plenty of time to recover."

"What about Rosie? Is she..."

"She's fine. I talked to Bryce just a little while ago. And you're going to have lots of help with her until you're feeling yourself again."

She was glad, but she wished she could see Rosie herself and hold her close right now.

A light knock at the door drew Jay over to open it. He motioned for Nate to come in.

Nate gave her hand a squeeze. "I'm so incredibly relieved that you're going to be okay. You gave us all quite a scare."

"I knew you guys would be there. Thank you both for saving my life." She looked from Jay to Nate. "Did you catch Carl?"

Nate nodded. "We did. And he immediately turned on Abbott once he was in custody."

Peyton gasped. "Detective Abbott?"

"Turns out he's been accepting money from a number of illegal businesses in town with the promise to make sure they continue to stay off the police department's radar. That included Cindy's restaurant. Once Trina stole the money, Cindy hired Bull to find it." Nate looked disgusted. "Patterson said it's all part of a bigger drug-running operation, but that's something the local police department is trying to sort out. They're still looking for Abbott. I can't imagine he'll be able to elude them for long."

"I just wish I knew why Trina stole the money in the first place."

Nate hesitated, and she could tell he knew something but wasn't sure it was the time tell her.

"What is it?"

Nate glanced at Jay, who gave him a nod.

"According to the initial investigation, it looks like Trina's boyfriend, Stephen Lewis, was practically drowning in gambling debt. We think she might have stolen the money initially to help him. We may never know whether she realized it was part of a laundering scheme or not. They closed in on her quickly, and she wasn't even able to give any of the money to Stephen before things went south."

Peyton blinked away the tears as sorrow filled her heart. She wanted to say the theory wasn't possible, but she knew better. Trina hated to be without a man, and she'd proven in the past that she'd do whatever she needed to in order to keep the current man of the month in her life.

Would Trina have resorted to stealing money for him so he'd feel indebted to her? Peyton couldn't deny it was possible.

But even though Trina hadn't made great decisions, she'd sacrificed herself in the end to protect Rosie. And that was how Peyton would choose to remember her.

Nate gave her a concerned look. "I think that's enough depressing talk for now. I just wanted to see for myself that you were okay. It's great to have you back with us, Peyton."

"It's great to *be* back. Thanks again for all you did."

He gave her a small nod and went back out the door, closing it again behind him.

Once again, Jay and Peyton had the room to themselves.

He settled in the chair beside the bed again. "What are you going to do once the doctors say you can leave?"

He spoke conversationally, but there was no missing the worry in his eyes. He wanted to know where she was going to go.

"My first priority is to find a new job and a place to live so that I can give Rosie the best life possible." She smiled wistfully. "But neither of us belongs in Houston. This has never felt like home to me." She watched his face, but there was nothing except openness to the conversation. "Did you mean what you said about wanting me in your life again?"

"Honey, my life is better with you in it. I just wish it hadn't taken so long to recognize that." There was no missing the regret and sincerity in his eyes.

"I want to come home, Jay. To Destiny." She reached out and placed her palm against his cheek. "To you."

He put his hand over hers and then held it against his heart. The quickened beats she felt there matched her own.

"There is nothing I want more." He brushed some hair out of her face and ran a finger down her cheek. "I love you, Peyton. I've never stopped loving you."

She reached for him then, slipping her fingers into the hair at the base of his neck. "I love you, too. I always have."

He leaned in and captured her lips in a kiss that promised a second chance at forever.

Epilogue
Three Months Later

Rosie sat on Peyton's lap. The moment Jay moved his hands away from his face and shouted, "Peek-a-boo!" the little girl erupted in laughter. She laughed so hard that she fell backward against Peyton's chest.

It didn't matter that the two of them had been playing this game for the last fifteen minutes. Every time Jay revealed a silly face with those words, Rosie's giggles followed. Which, of course, made Peyton laugh, too. How could she not?

Jay sat next to them on their couch and turned toward them so their knees touched. They'd be heading over to Bryce and Megan's house soon. Peyton had made dinner to take, and she couldn't wait to get her hands on sweet little Alexander Bryce. The baby had made his appearance last month with his daddy's blue eyes and his mommy's dimples.

Jay surprised Peyton when he used his free arm as a hook around her waist and drew her close. He claimed her lips in a kiss that left her heart thundering in her chest. If it hadn't been for a squirming baby on her lap and somewhere to go in a few minutes, it would have been so easy to get lost in his touch.

When he broke the kiss—much sooner than Peyton would have preferred—he sighed. He lifted her left hand and pressed a kiss to the wedding ring on her finger.

Once they'd known that they belonged together, they hadn't seen any reason to wait. They got married the last week of October in a small, simple ceremony that included family and close friends. It'd been hard for Peyton not to have her sister there with her, but everyone had been supportive and loving.

Rosie reached for Jay, and he took her in his arms and nuzzled her cheek. "She's growing so fast. It's hard to keep up with her. She'll be crawling all over the place before long."

Peyton groaned. "Don't remind me." She laughed.

Jay lovingly ran a hand over the baby's curly hair. He turned his attention to Peyton, and his eyes glinted mischievously. "You know, I think Rosie would enjoy having a little cousin to play with."

"Hmm... Do you, now?"

"Most definitely." Jay leaned in until his lips nearly touched her ear. "I think I'd enjoy it, too."

Peyton's cheeks heated, but she couldn't keep the smile from her face. "You are something else."

"Yeah, but I'm *your* something else."

Praise God that He saw fit to give them another chance together. All she'd needed to do was stop running from the past so that she could build a new future with the man who was the other half of her heart.

This time, Peyton leaned in for a kiss.

"Forever and always."

Special Thanks

I want to send a special shout-out to my friends, Elizabeth and Rachel, for all of the brainstorming. Your thoughts and suggestions were so helpful when it came to writing this book.

Many thanks to my editor, Erynn, for her awesomeness. This book wouldn't be the same without you.

Denny and Steph, thank you for always taking the time to read early copies and catch those pesky typos that like to sneak through. Love you ladies!

To the members of my ARC team: You guys are amazing. Between sharing new releases, spotting typos, and your encouragement, you are truly rock stars in my book. I can't tell you how much I appreciate each of you.

Most of all, I want to thank my Heavenly Father for the opportunity to continue to do what I love so much.

About the Author

Melanie D. Snitker is a *USA Today* bestselling author who writes inspirational romance and romantic suspense. She and her husband live in Texas with their two children. They share their home with three dogs and two terrariums filled with small critters. In her spare time, Melanie enjoys photography, reading, training her dog, playing computer games, and hanging out with family and friends.

https://www.melaniedsnitker.com/

facebook.com/melaniedsnitker

x.com/MelanieDSnitker

instagram.com/melaniedsnitker

bookbub.com/authors/melanie-d-snitker

goodreads.com/melaniedsnitker

Books by Melanie D. Snitker

Danger in Destiny

Out of the Ashes

Frozen in Jeopardy

Beneath the Surface

Caught in the Crosshairs

Running from the Past

In Search of the Truth

Assigned to Protect

Brides of Clearwater

Marrying Mandy

Marrying Raven

Marrying Chrissy

Marrying Bonnie

Marrying Emma

Marrying Noel

Books by Melanie D. Snitker